Shoreline

Science fiction magazine from Scotland

ISSN 2059-2590
ISBN 978-1-9997002-0-1

Shoreline of Infinity is available in digital or print editions.
Submissions of fiction, art, reviews, poetry, non-fiction are welcomed:
visit the website to find out how to submit.

www.shorelineofinfinity.com

Publisher
Shoreline of Infinity Publications / The New Curiosity Shop
Edinburgh
Scotland

280517

Contents

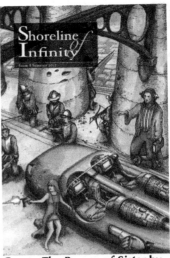

Cover: *The Rescue of Sister* by
Stephen Pickering

Editorial Team
Editor & Editor-in-Chief:
Noel Chidwick

Art Director:
Mark Toner

Deputy Editor & Poetry Editor:
Russell Jones

Reviews Editor:
Iain Maloney

Assistant Editor & First Reader:
Monica Burns

*Copy editors:*Iain Maloney,
Russell Jones, Andrew J Wilson

Extra thanks to: Caroline
Grebbell, M Luke McDonell,
Katy Lennon, Abbie Waters

Congratulations to Barnaby Seddon (age 7)
who won our Eastercon joke competition with:

Q – What do you do if you see a spaceman?

A – You park in it man.

Barnaby, you will go far!

First Contact

www.shorelineofinfinity.com

contact@shorelineofInfinity.com

Twitter: @shoreinf

and on Facebook

Pull up a Log

We have another fine crop of story-tellers and poets for you in this issue. There's a wee tale of what threatens to be from Eric Brown (his novel, *The Kings of Eternity*, is on my reading list equivalent of speed-dial). We have an elegant story from Jeannette Ng of a sacrifice in an Aztec Cyberpunk Dystopia. Barry Charman writes of isolation and ambition – on a stellar scale; Laura Duerr tests us with a gruesome temptation; Premee Mohamed offers a raw tale of love under fire in an alien war; Michael Teasdale leads us on a spiralling journey into a crumbling reality; and Nathan Susnik hints at what happens when reality is ignored. Chris Kelso, our contemporary writer featured in SF Caledonia, takes us through anguish with the help of a time machine.

When we gather stories for an issue, we don't look for a theme, but one often emerges. And this issue belies the nonsense that science fiction is just about ray guns and aliens*: it's people in circumstances that test their humanity, challenge their very being.

And so we come to another aim of *Shoreline of Infinity* – to encourage you to grab a sheaf of blank paper and demonstrate your penskills. We have a flash fiction competition to tide you over the summer months, with a pair of pictures waiting for their stories to be told.

But before you do, make sure you read Ruth EJ Booth's *The Legend of the Kick-Arse Wise Women* to set you on your way: "I began to write in earnest. And once I did, things began to change."

Settle in and enjoy the ride.

Noel Chidwick
Editor-in-chief
Shoreline of Infinity
June 2017

* though sometimes ray guns and aliens are just what you need to get you through the day.

The Pink Life

(La Vie En Rose)

Nathan Susnik

Art: Dave Alexander

On **Monday a crisply painted** fire hydrant moved into the alcove next to my apartment building. On Tuesday it sang *La Boheme*. On Wednesday, *Carmen*. Today, *Der Vogelfänger*. The fire hydrant has digitally perfect tone and tenor. I walk past it twice a day on my way to work:

#operasingingfirehydrant #pureperfection

I reach my 85th floor office, greet my secretary, and look out at the architecture. The city is an art deco wonderland. #newyork1950s. Market reports waterfall down the Chrysler Building, splashing onto the Theatre des Champs-Elysees. A personal message blinks on the Empire State Building:

@rickstock538 – InComp/Filefunk merger approved. Buy!

I'm halfway through a reply when – flash – #newyork1950s is gone. An endless field of homogeneous, concrete skyscrapers is in its place.

Flash – #newyork1950s.

Flash – endless concrete skyscrapers.

Flash – #newyork1950s.

Flash. Flash. Flash.

"Ava," I say.

"Yes Ms. van Kamp?" She comes in the room looking different from before, less than perfect. There's a pimple on her forehead, a large white head pressing out from a glowing red base.

Flash – Silky smooth.

Flash – Krakatoa.

"What do you see outside?" I say. She ambles to the window, limping slightly. She shrugs.

"Buildings?"

"Nothing unusual?"

"Nothing," she says.

"Thank you Ava. You can go." I sigh.

#whyisitalwaysme

When she leaves, I message Dsense corp. Five seconds later (poof) they project a representative over the intercerebral computer.

"It's not an error with the iPerceive app. It must be a problem with your operating system ma'am," she says. "Turn iPerceive off."

"You can do that?"

"Do what?"

"Turn iPerceive off," I say. She winks.

"You'd be surprised how many people don't know that. But then again, why in God's name, would you want to turn it off? Anyway, if you have it on while it's glitching, it can be dangerous."

"Dangerous?"

"Yes, just between you and me, a client jumped in Niagra Falls last year thinking the water was cotton candy. Anyway, have the InComp run an update tonight while you sleep. That should solve the problem."

"I'm not paying for services this month," I say.

She is as sweet as strawberries. "Here at Dsense corp customer satisfaction is key. You won't be charged for services for the next two months. Plus we'll..." She pauses, scanning through her records, trying to find an app or addon that I don't have. "...we'll unlock AllGourmet level 5 for two months."

"Fine," I say.

I stare out the window. The shadows of concrete monstrosities darken the streets below. It's depressing, like being smothered with a soiled pillow.

"Serotonin levels decreasing. Go ahead and take the day off," advises LifeCoach app. It's good advice, and I should follow it.

Since subscribing to LifeCoach my self-satisfaction levels have increased 523%, according to LifeCoach app. A message blinks from the dark streets:

@rickstock538: U buy?

I exhale, and LifeCoach tells me about the dangers of critically low neurotransmitters.

@laurenvankamp923: Technical problems, Plz take account till 2morrow! #vactionday

✳

I board a transporter. Without iPerceive, darkness fills streets where sunlight formerly shone. There are considerably fewer flowers than usual, considerably fewer birds too. In fact, I realise, no birds and no flowers; it's all trash and beggars, concrete and darkness.

I get home, and in the place of the #operasingingfirehydrant is a beggar. He's young, the left half of his face is scar tissue, his eyes are sunken, and his cheek bones are too sharp. Instead of singing opera, he's begging. He wants food. A wave of crumminess sweeps over me. LifeCoach calmly informs me about dangerous levels of something or other. I flip iPerceive back on.

Flash – *The Barber of Seville.*

Flash – homeless beggar.

Flash – Count Almaviva.

Flash – beggar.

iDentify kicks in:

*Ping – *Sergeant Steven Johnson, 32, earned a Silver Star and a Purple Heart in the second battle of Pyongyang...*

I interrupt the facial recognition app. Wait, a *second* battle of Pyongyang? When did that happen?

*Ping – *The Second battle of Pyongyang began on April...*

I interrupt WikiSearch app. On second thought, I really don't need to know.

Sergeant Johnson looks at me. He cocks his head like some kind of intelligent bird. It's clicked. He knows that I see him.

"Please," he says reaching out. I walk past. He follows. "I'm hungry," he says. I keep walking. He reaches to touch my shoulder. I jump away and he screams, grabbing his head. I exhale. At least ProTect app is still functional.

"I'm sorry. I didn't mean to scare you," says the beggar, but I am up the stairs and in the building.

I lay on the sofa, head spinning, waiting for sleep. I post #badday and there is a wave of #sosorrys, what's wrong?s, #poorbabys, Kitten pix, Puppy pix, Frowny faces, inspirational quotes, and #feels on my wall. An email pings in. It's from my mother. Subj: Opportunity/joys of motherhood. There's an attachment, an advertisement for a surrogacy firm.

#notreadymom. I need updates. I turn DreamWell, and (poof) I'm out, dreaming an archived file.

The shop is old. My grandfather picks up something large and square. Dust flies, and I sneeze. "I remember these. My grandfather had these," he says chuckling. "Watch this." He pulls a black circle from the rectangle, puts it on something and flips a switch. The circle spins around and around. There's a noise like fingernails on wood. Then, music starts. There's no digital fixing, no lyrical translation, no tempo control; it's scratchy and all treble, the woman's voice is too shrill and in a language that I don't understand. The song melancholy but joyous, sober but whimsical, flawed but... (poof) DreamWell pulls me into the next archived file. But there's something about the song, and I want to linger, to listen. DreamWell won't let me. Dwelling in files leads to obsession, and obsession leads to bad sleep, and bad sleep leads to low levels of something or other. LifeCoach works in concert with DreamWell and I'm pulled into the next archived file, then the next and the next, until I wake up in the morning, fully refreshed

I roll off of the sofa, LifeCoach playing a light piano ditty in the background. "You have 165 new notifications, none of them urgent," it says. "Have patience, you can check the notification underway to work. For now, enjoy the perfect morning." I look out the window. Sunlight glints off of a pristine layer of snow coving my Art Deco wonderland.

#snow #newyork1950s #pureperfection

ProGusto has huevos rancheros ready and waiting in the kitchen.

AllGourmet level 5, #wow #pureperfection #timeforwork

Opening the door, I see people passing on the sidewalk, their feet leaving no impressions in the immaculate whiteness. I listen to the virgin snow, crunch, crunch, crunching beneath my feet as I walk down the stairs. It's the only sound in this muted, winter wonderland, and...

And something is missing, something that was here yesterday, but not today.

Opera music.

I find the crisply painted fire hydrant tucked into a corner of the alcove.

"Hello?" I say. It doesn't respond. "The snow is beautiful. Why aren't you singing today?" I ask. The hydrant remains silent. There's something wrong. It should be singing, moving, doing something.

"Hey," I say. "Hey?"

"Everything alright?" interrupts a voice from above me.

*Ping – *Juan da Silva Torrão, 47, lives in apartment 12J.*

He peers down into the alcove at me. I know what he's thinking.

#losingit #crazy

"Yeah. I just dropped something," I say.

"Okay," he says and walks down the stairs, foot prints disappearing as he goes.

The fire hydrant remains still, just sitting there as if frozen stiff.

Frozen stiff.

But it's not that cold, is it?

"Heart rate increasing, blood pressure rising. Time for a break," says LifeCoach. It starts playing a light piano ditty again. *The best choice is to just walk away. Don't get involved,* I think. *Just call the city. They'll send someone out in a jiffy to pick it up.*

It...

I take a step away from the fire hydrant.

Crunch, goes my foot into the immaculate white sheet.

A second crunch.

Five more. Crunch, crunch, crunch, crunch, crunch. I turn. My foot prints are gone. There's only virgin snow between the fire hydrant and me. No trail of incrimination. I could leave now. When I come home later, (poof) the problem will simply disappear as readily as my footsteps.

"Blood pressure..."

I interrupt LifeCoach. Is he really frozen or just acting? It this some pity game he's playing to get free food? Before yesterday, I didn't know he existed. But now I've seen. Now I know what's in that corner, cold and not moving. Oh God.

#terriblebadnogoodstupidstupidstupididea

But I have to.

As iPerceive shuts down, sunlight turns to shadow, pure snow turns to trodden slush and the silent hydrant turns to a shivering man, curled under a blanket in the only dry corner, and I...

#waitaminute

Shivering?

He's alive?

"Your heart rate is..." I interrupt LifeCoach and run to him.

"Hey..." I say. I've forgotten his name. He looks at me.

*Ping – *Sergeant Steven Johnson*

"Hey Steven," I say. "You're freezing," He nods. "You need help." He nods. "Okay, okay, okay, okay," I say.

"Epinephrine and norepinephrine critical. Anxiety is a health hazard. Relax, put your feet up. Imagine a happy place," says LifeCoach and starts a steel-drum-Caribbean ditty.

"Go to hell," I say, but the steel-drum ditty keeps playing. Sergeant Johnson's eyes widen. "No, no, no, not you. Don't go to hell. I was talking to LifeCoach," I say.

"L-l-l-i-i-f-f?" he stammers.

"Never mind," I say. But I still don't know what to do.

13

*Ping — *Treatment of hypothermia. Bring the victim to a warm place. Remove wet clothing. Wrap the victim in a blanket. Bring the victim a warm drink...*

#thankgodforwikisearch

I drape St. Johnson over my shoulder and wretch, twice. I've never smelled anything like him. My knees buckle as I take the first stair. I take the next two with my hand on the concrete.

Three stairs up, I hear:

"Lauren, I was just going by on my way to the office." I turn. Who is this bald man speaking to me? "Listen, I wanted to talk to you," he says. "I was able to catch the tail the action, but we missed out on most of the profit from the merger yesterday."

*Ping — *Rick Stock. Business Associate. Twitter: @rickstock538*

#OMG.

It's Rick, but it's not Rick. It's like Rick's chubby older brother.

"Okay, yeah. The merger," I grunt. Why doesn't he offer to help?

"Well, the problem is that this mistake is probably going to cost the company a pretty penny. This might be reflected in your bonus and..." I stumble. He cocks his head, "Is this a bad time?"

"I think that I need another day off," I say. Rick peers at the homeless man on my shoulder, opens his mouth and then closes it.

"Alright," he finally says. "It's your bonus, not mine." He turns to go and then stops. "Just out of curiosity, is this some kind of modern art or something?"

"Modern art?" I say, the steel-drum ditty in my head still going de-dada, da-da-da, do-do-do-do-do, de-de da-da-da.

"The fire hydrant," he says pointing at my shoulder.

"Oh, yeah," I say. "Modern art."

"You know that there's a new neo-perfectionist exhibit that you might be interested in. It's over on... (*Ping) ...Kinnickinnic Avenue," he says.

"Great, I'll check it out," I say.

"Alright," he says. "Enjoy your day off. See you tomorrow." Then, he trots down the slushy, dark sidewalk, cheerily whistling the same steel-drum-Caribbean ditty playing in my head.

Inside, I put Sergeant Johnson on the sofa.

*Ping — *Remove wet clothing. Wrap victim in a blanket.*

I do what WikiSearch tells me to. It's, well...unpleasant.

*Ping — *Bring victim a warm drink.*

I run to the kitchen. AutoBev pours a nice cup of, water?

#wtf

I asked for hot coco. Okay then, tea.

It's water.

Coffee = water.

Mulled wine = water.

Merlot = water.

Beer = water.

Coco loco = water.

Vodka? Water.

Talk about timing. My AutoBev is broken. I'm halfway through a message to the repair department when it hits me.

iPerceive on.

Suddenly, the kitchen is a gustatory wonderland, full of multicolored hot/cold/sweet/bitter/fizzy/flat/flamboyant drinks. I sip the vodka.

#burnssogood

I gulp it down, the whole cup. It's exactly what I need right now. There's a pleasant tingling in my stomach and fingers. My head drifts off like a balloon.

"Excuse me?" I hear from the other room.

iPerceive off. My head is clear as a bell.

Hmm...

On, buzzed.

Off, sober.

On, off, on, off, on/off/on/off/on/off.

"Hello?" calls Sergeant Johnson.

"Just a minute," I call back, grabbing the hot cocoa/water. Oh yeah, it's not even warm. It gets dumped in the disposal. I run to the bathroom, shove the cup under the shower head and hope. Yes! It's warm.

#thankgod

Stg. Johnson is sitting on my sofa, shivering. I hold out the cup and he takes it.

"Thank you," he says. "There's no need to panic. I'll be fine. I've seen worse." He looks at me, and sees me shaking worse than he is. "Really, I'll be fine," he adds.

"Look," I say. "This isn't a free ride. You can stay and get warm. I'll even get you something to eat, but then you have to go somewhere else."

"Where?" he says.

"I don't know. I'll find for you a place at a shelter or something. Is there anything else I can do for you right now?" I say.

"Yes," he says. "Tell me your name."

#impossible

He must not have any apps, not even a rudimentary like iDentify.

"Lauren Van Kamp," I say.

"Thank you, Ms. Van Kamp," he says and then lies back down on the sofa.

While he sleeps, I InComp the city shelter. (Poof) Suddenly I'm standing in a concert hall sized room. It's stacked from floor to ceiling with occupied beds.

#cordwood

"Hello," says a worker. He's grey-haired and has bags under his eyes. iDentify tells me his name. I ask him if there's a free bed. He says no. I offer a small bribe. He says no. I offer a moderate bribe. "That's enough to afford LifeCoach. It looks like you could use it," I say. He laughs, then says that it doesn't matter how much I offer. The shelter is full. He clarifies:

#atcapacity

#wayovercapacity, actually. He takes me outside and shows me a crowd of hundreds of people. They're all waiting for a meal.

When did this happen?

*Ping – *Poverty has been on a steady incline since...*

I interrupt WikiSearch. This is another one of those things that I really don't need to know. Fuck, why haven't I seen this before. I flip iPerceive on.

A flock of storks...

#jesuschrist, that's why.

I flip iPerceive off. "I'm sorry, but there's nothing I can do," says the grey-haired man.

"Goodbye," I say, hanging up and shaking my head.

Sitting in my living room, I bury my head in my hands. LifeCoach tells me of my serotonin levels, suggest a day at the spa, offers wonderful holidays, real and virtual, and tells me that my self-satisfaction levels have dropped 452%, in a single hour. They're the lowest since I have gotten the app. I can't think, so I shut it off. I'd give anything for an #operasingingfirehydrant, for my #newyork1950s, for my #pureperfection, to forget.

I search the Dsense corp app store. There it is: GuiltFree. It promises to erase most of the last two days, but it's out of my price range. Maybe with my bonus...

#shit

I missed the merger, which means goodbye bonus.

※

For lunch, my ProGusto cooks filet mignon with mashed potatoes. The two dishes are actually some type of grey protein slurry, just with different constancies.

Sergeant Johnson is up and off of the couch. He's in a good mood and wolfs the protein slurry down like it really is filet mignon. I turn on iPerceive and pick at my food while watching the crisply-painted fire hydrant across the table from me. It's not moving, but the food slowly disappears.

The fire hydrant starts singing. "Huh," I say, turning iPerceive off.

"Is it supposed to be cold tonight?" he asks.

Very cold, but I don't tell him that. It's one of those things that he doesn't need to know. Instead, I say:

"There's no room at the shelter."

"Yeah," he says.

"And I can't keep you here," I say.

"I know," he says. He finishes his meal, gets up and slowly walks to the door, dragging his feet. He opens the door, turns and says, "Thank you." Then he smiles, scarred lip peeling back to reveal missing and rotten teeth. And there's something about the smile. It's not ugly. It's like the song, the one from my DreamWell archive, the one my grandfather played on the disc in the antique shop, melancholy but joyous, sober but whimsical, flawed but... real, something that I could touch, something I could feel, something created, existing only for a moment, shared between two human beings. It's not perfect; it's beautiful. Sergeant Johnson turns and leaves, shutting the door behind him.

I sit on the couch thinking about Sergeant Johnson. I play with iPerceive, flipping it on, turning it off, turning it back on, then back off. On, off, on, off, on/off/on. Now I'm at the door, now outside; now it's snowing again, cold and getting colder. I turn iPerceive off. I follow muddy tracks in the virgin snow.

Nathan Susnik. is a biomedical researcher and medical writer who lives with his wife and children in Hanover, Germany. His fiction has appeared on *Gallery of Curiosities* and is forthcoming from in *Devilfish Review* and *Grievous Angel*. For publication updates, follow him on Twitter at @NathanSusnik.

ONE COG TURNING By Anthony Laken

Bellina Ressa, daughter of the Lord Chancellor, has lived a sheltered life. Shunned by the rest of the nobility due to her Cognopathic abilities, she has become strong willed and independent. But in the blink of an eye, she finds herself betrothed to the arrogant Elvgren Lovitz and on a diplomatic mission to save the Estrian empire.

Joined on this perilous quest by her fiancé and the resolute Major Cirona Bouchard, Bellina is about to discover that intrigue lurks just beneath the surface and danger lies in wait around every corner.

One Cog Turning is a rip-roaring new Steampunk adventure, featuring a cast of foul-mouthed, irreverent and memorable oddballs.

JOIN US FOR THE BOOK LAUNCH ON SATURDAY 15/07 AT EDGE-LIT!

COME RAISE A GLASS WITH US AND HELP CELEBRATE ANTHONY'S FIRST EVER BOOK LAUNCH!

www.lunapresspublishing.com

The Black Tide

Laura Duerr

Art: P Emerson Williams

The harvest moon drew us out to the beach late on Friday night. It was mid-September, still warm, and I ached to escape campus with my new friends and enjoy the coast – no matter the hour – before the autumn rains started. I sat in the back of Angela's Jeep with Gabe. Up front, Angela and Kate argued over the best route to take.

"Michelle, you grew up there," Angela said as we left campus. "Which freeway do we want?"

"It's almost midnight – does it matter?"

"Fair."

We reached the beach within an hour and a half, expecting to find the town asleep, but it was as crowded as a summer weekend. Every street, every parking lot, even front yards and dunes were crammed with cars. Shadowy masses of shouting people poured down the moonlit, sandy lanes towards the beach. I'd hoped for the head-clearing solitude of the deserted coast; instead, the atmosphere felt more like the minutes before a concert starts, all electric anticipation.

Much too late, I remembered why. The moonlight should have reminded me, but I'd worked so hard to forget. It had felt so freeing, so daring, to mark up my September calendar with normal things like soccer practice and homework due dates instead of the countdown to the harvest moon – but there it was, gleaming innocently, luring all these people down to the surf.

I felt two truths instantly: the moon would take my new friends, and it would be my fault – unless I did something.

"Maybe we should just try again next weekend," I suggested. It was the best I could come up with. I couldn't tell them the truth, they'd think I was crazy, but in my panic, I couldn't think fast enough.

"No way." Angela continued down another block, negotiating the Jeep through the swarming crowds. "I didn't drive all the way out here just to turn around."

Her bangles jingled against the steering wheel. My dresser top was scattered with orphaned earrings and a tangle of necklaces, but Angela's looked like a store display, with dainty metal trees showcasing her jewelry. Angela asked weekly if I'd help keep the room clean, but I kept finding excuses – I had practice, I had homework, I was late for class. I'd found excuses to let Gabe take on more than his fair share of work for our case study. I'd even found excuses to avoid Kate when she needed someone to talk to about missing her boyfriend. I'd been selfish and I'd taken my friends for granted. After tonight, that would change. We just needed to get back to campus.

But no excuse seemed good enough, especially since I'd been the one to suggest the adventure – we had no game tomorrow, no need to go to bed early.

I felt sick – and then relieved. I opened my mouth to say I wasn't feeling well, to beg them to drive me home. "Look!" Kate pointed. "Those guys are leaving."

Three people climbed slowly into their sedan. They were crying.

"What's that about?" Gabe wondered. I said nothing. They wouldn't believe me anyway, and if they refused to leave, they would find out soon enough.

When the sedan didn't immediately depart, Kate reached over and tapped the horn, earning us a trio of middle fingers.

"Just give them a minute," I burst out.

"Jesus, fine – I just want to get out of this car, already."

The sedan left and Angela took its space. Kate had already unbuckled and leaped out before the engine shut off. Within moments, I was alone in the car.

"Let's go!" Kate shouted.

The sounds outside were familiar, the soundtrack to my annual living nightmare. As I climbed down from the Jeep, I felt like I was five, or twelve, or fifteen again, terrified of how my quiet beach town turned into a moonlit hell once a year.

The streets were raucous with voices and the distant surf. The thrum fed Kate like a breath over embers, but for me, it was a harrowing reminder of why I'd left. I'd chosen a college inland, safe from the moon, but also near enough to reach my family, if needed. Every past harvest moon night loomed in my mind: identical memories of trying and failing to sleep, thanks to the blinding full moon and the shouts of triumph and grief that reverberated through the town all night.

I wanted to run, to hide in the car where it was safe – but I knew if I let my friends out of my sight, I might lose them forever. They didn't know, and even those who knew were lost so easily on nights like this.

So I caught up with them as they ran the final block to the beach. Kate led the way. Her blonde ponytail danced as she dodged between eager visitors pressing towards the ocean and wild-eyed mourners leaving.

"What the hell are so many people doing here?" Gabe asked as a sobbing woman collided with him and drifted away. "And why are so many of them crying?"

I almost told him. If I could catch them one by one and explain it to them, there was a chance they'd believe me and agree to leave – but then we reached the dunes.

Even Kate fell silent at the sight of the beach. The pale sands were coated in black. Hordes of people with flashlights crisscrossed the beach, so many that their voices almost drowned out the surf, the flashlight beams slicing across the pitch-dark sands. The noise was alternately hellish and jubilant.

"Was there an oil spill or something?" Angela asked.

"It's the black tide." All three stared at me. "Once a year, during the harvest moon, millions of black jellies wash ashore. No one's ever been able to figure out what they are, or even if they're alive or dead. We just call it the black tide. My parents always kept me inside whenever they came ashore."

"Why?" Kate kept glancing back to the crowds. "Because of all the crazy people?"

"Because of the jellies themselves; because one time, ages ago, people tried eating them." My stomach turned, roiled by fear and disgust. "About half of them died instantly. Just dropped dead where they stood."

24

Kate wrinkled her nose. "And the other half?"

"They're probably still here," I said. "They lived forever."

They stared at me for a moment, then Gabe barked a laugh. "Come on. Is that your town's version of the Jersey Devil story or something?"

"It's true." I pointed. "Just watch them. They cluster around each other and egg each other on and wind each other up until finally someone is brave enough to pick one up and try it. They come with friends and family and they all swear they'll keep each other from doing something stupid, but secretly they hope it'll work, that they'll be one of the chosen ones. And then they'll go home with a parent or a sibling or a spouse who will never die...or they'll go home alone. Just watch them."

We inched down the dunes, afraid to get close to that slimy black mass but drawn by its possibility. Though I knew I shouldn't, though the thought made me shudder, I wanted to touch one, to finally understand what made them so tempting.

A man, his triumphant face lit by a half-dozen flashlights, dragged the blade of a pocket knife across his bare chest. Blood poured down, but the wound sealed itself in the blade's wake. Angela gagged; Kate gaped. I covered my mouth and found my cheeks were wet: I was crying. For all I knew, I had been crying since I saw the tide.

"I didn't know it was tonight." Was I asking preemptively for forgiveness? Or was I praying, or perhaps planning what I would say to the parents of whoever might succumb to the temptation? "If I'd known it was tonight, I'd never have let us come out here."

"Don't worry about it. None of us are stupid enough to take that risk," Angela said.

"Really? I was going to say none of us are stupid enough to turn it down." Gabe stooped and came up with a handful of jewel-black organisms. I lashed out reflexively and struck his wrist before he could fully straighten up, sending the black spots spattering.

But it was too late: the crowd, alert for anyone making the attempt, gathered tight around. Led by the newly immortal man with the bloody chest, they pressed in. My feet were stepped on and an elbow jabbed my side. No apologies followed: their attention – their will, even – was fixed on Gabe.

"Are you going to do it?" The hushed insistence came swiftly, an uninterrupted susurrus of temptation, the voice of the Serpent itself. "He's gonna do it. Is it worth the risk? Do it, man. What've you got to lose?"

One last bit of black slime still clung to Gabe's index finger. He squinted at it, turning it to catch the light from the jittery flashlights. I was too far away to stop him. He tossed his head, making his bangs dance to one side: his nervous tic whenever he didn't know the answer to a question.

"I mean," he said softly, "I'm only 18. I haven't done jack, so it's not like it would be a waste. On the other hand...I haven't done jack *yet*. That's worth living for."

"But you could have forever to do it." I recognized the woman who spoke. Her name was Nancy and she had been 33 since before my parents were born. She liked to demo her immortality by letting visitors shoot her in the head. In lean years, she charged ten dollars each for the opportunity.

I hated her.

Gabe raised his finger.

I couldn't reach him, but I couldn't cry out, either – my throat was frozen, clenched tight. I hated the tide, I hated Nancy, I hated myself.

Fresh screams broke out just a few feet away. I jumped. The flashlights swept off Gabe and cast a white circle on a gray-haired woman cradling the body of a younger woman. The daughter's eyes were brown. They stared up at the moonlit sky, her face a death mask of desperate hope.

Safe in the shadows, Gabe flicked the black from his finger.

"Let's get out of here." Angela touched his shoulder and drew him away from the force of the hissing circle. "Grab Kate. We're going."

I felt a fresh churn of panic. "I don't see her."

Fresh cheers erupted, closer to the waves. Angela led us toward the sound, and sure enough, there was Kate. Somehow she'd gotten a flashlight and now she stood in the front lines of a crowd which surrounded eight people, each lit by flashlights like performers on a stage. Each pinched a sliver of black between their fingers. The crowd – Kate, too – was chanting, faster and faster, a single syllable: *Eat! Eat! Eat!*

The hands went up, the heads whipped back, throats convulsed, and five people dropped to the sand. The crowd rippled as individuals broke loose to weep over the dead, while the three victors turned, fists raised to roars of triumph. Their relieved loved ones embraced them; awestruck onlookers unwilling to take the risk themselves reached out to touch the newly immortal.

I expected Kate to be one of them, but I couldn't see her in the crazed paths of the flashlights. I saw Nancy, though, laughing and kissing the cheeks of the survivors. Her neck and chest gleamed red, and I remembered how Dad said some years she let people slit her throat instead of shooting her.

The crowd shifted, seeking the next attempt. I knew there would be many more tonight; I remembered how few of my classmates still had both parents, their grandparents, their teachers. As we got older, we lost each other, too: the high school lost three in one year when I was a sophomore.

I also remembered how many spouses outlived not only their partners, but their children. I remembered Mallory Watkins, who waited until she turned 18 to try the tide and was rewarded with eternal youth.

Somehow, I could still see Nancy. She seemed to be everywhere, like a good hostess, but no matter where I looked, I couldn't find Kate.

I turned back to tell the others. Only Gabe was there. I opened my mouth to scream for Angela, but she emerged from the crowd, her face set.

"We're going back to the car."

"What about Kate?"

"She says she'll meet us there."

"We can't leave her here! She could—"

"Any of us could," Angela snapped. "Gabe almost did. You might; I might. I'm not sticking around. Back to the car. I'm leaving in fifteen minutes, with or without you."

She shoved back through the crowds up the dunes. I took Gabe's arm.

"Let's go."

"We're not seriously leaving Kate?"

"The longer we stay here, the more danger we're in. We have to go now, or we never will."

27

Gabe was pale in the moonlight. He looked around one more time; whether for Kate or for another shot at the black tide, I couldn't tell. At last, he sighed and let me lead him up the beach. I kept my eyes on my feet, trying to avoid stepping in the slimy patches of black and the occasional splash of the immortals' blood. The laughter and screaming made my ears ring.

Eventually clumps of dune grass replaced the black tide, and the slope led us up to safety. Angela stood at the top, arms folded like a general surveying the aftermath of battle.

"How the hell did you grow up here?" she asked.

I couldn't answer.

The crowds weren't diminishing; the force of them pressing towards the beach was like a second tide. We wove through it. I felt lighter and yet more anxious with every step. We were almost safe. We might make it out.

We might – but Kate might not. The twist in my stomach returned. I didn't want to leave her, but I didn't ever want to see the bloody, black-smeared beach again.

At last, the Jeep appeared. We each clambered in, locked our door, and sat in the darkness, waiting. My ears still rang.

Angela's eyes were dull, her ochre skin made wan and grim by the yellow streetlamps. "Nine minutes."

Gabe shook his head. "We should go back down."

"Don't," I whispered. "Don't go back out there."

Someone pounded on my window and we shrieked. It was a young man, our age, flexing his arms and sticking his tongue out in a grotesque victory dance. His friends pounded his back in celebration. One hung back, quiet

"They lost someone," I said softly.

The boys moved on. I wondered what school they went to.

"Eight minutes," Angela murmured.

"I snuck down once," I said. The confession burst out of me – I'd never told anyone before. I didn't even want to tell my friends, not really, but even this was better than the silence. "I was thirteen. The black tide was common knowledge in our town, but my parents refused to talk about it. I guess they thought if they never brought it up, I'd forget about it."

Angela scoffed. "How could anyone forget this?"

"I'd heard screams every fall since I was a baby. I guess I hoped it was fake, or exaggerated, so I went to see for myself. I planned to just touch one, just to see what it felt like, but then I saw..."

Nancy smiling, 33 forever, with a gun to her head; a flash, and the loudest noise. Blind, frozen panic while the eyes readjust, then Nancy again, holding the bullet, still smiling through the shining blood that coated her face.

"You saw what we saw," Angela filled in.

"I was so afraid, I never even touched it. I refused to go to the beach at all for months. I thought the slime must stick to the sand, and I was afraid of the sand getting in my mouth and killing me."

"Or making you live forever?"

"Gabe, Jesus, let it go." Angela glared in the rearview mirror.

"You guys never touched it," he said. "Once it's in your hand, you just think, why not?"

I considered telling him, challenging him to continue to think that way after hearing how, as an eighth-grader, I'd seen a woman shoot herself in the head and then laugh about it. Angela was right, though: they'd all seen more or less the same thing tonight. If Gabe was still tempted, another gruesome anecdote wouldn't reach him.

I would never forget, but maybe they still could.

"You made the right choice, Gabe," I said firmly.

He nodded, but said nothing.

Silence returned. Occasionally shrill cries cut into the car. I could no longer distinguish between the ecstatic and the desolate.

Gabe squinted into the crowd. "Is that her?"

I twisted in my seat. A blonde girl made her way towards the car, walking slowly.

"It's Kate!"

Angela unlocked the doors and started the engine. The brake lights illuminated Kate's face. She was smiling.

Laura Duerr is a writer and social media coordinator from Vancouver, Washington. She has a BA in Creative Writing from Linfield College. Her other stories have appeared in *Mad Scientist Journal* and the anthologies *Candlesticks & Daggers: An Anthology of Mixed-Genre Mysteries* and *Fitting In: Historical Accounts of Paranormal Subcultures*.

The Starchitect

Barry Charman

When he'd first presented Evie with the design, she'd told him it was impossible. But he'd smiled, like he knew she wouldn't be able to resist the challenge, the unprecedented task.

A year to the day he was heading to the "house" to pick up the keys.

She smiled at the terminology, it helped her retain a sense of scale. After all, what she'd done here was as much madness as science.

Evie watched from her monitor as Karl's shuttle ferried him down the Lightbridge. He would be alone here, after she'd gone.

Her engineers had worked miracles to do this. Karl's last message had said he'd pay her double for hitting his craziest deadline. He was already paying her more than she could quite comprehend.

The Lightbridge danced on the screen, a beam of pure white energy phased against an obsidian background – the only way the screen could even attempt to relay the information.

When she was gone, he would deactivate it and be cut off for all time.

She tried to remember how the structure had appeared to her on entry: a dark marble tower inside of six force walls that kept the radiation out.

So beautiful.

The docking lights flashed on the terminal, telling her he was in the hatch. She looked around the white room she'd just finished decorating. Filled with books, sculptures, paintings – some landscapes, but mostly of women – such a civilised cave to be walled up in.

It was hard to feel she hadn't just wallpapered in echoes.

She watched the cameras as he entered the airlock. His spacesuit was completely black, and its tinted visor left you practically blind. The suit did most of the walking. On the schematics it provided, he'd have had some concept of the building as he'd approached, some understanding of the massive undertaking they'd completed.

That was important, that their work be acknowledged. No one had attempted anything like this before, she couldn't just forget that.

She still had questions, but his motivations were none of her business. She couldn't forget *that*, either.

Evie watched as he left the airlock, and started to remove his suit. Karl Hauser. She remembered their first meeting, in his hotel room on Europa. A hundred and fifth floor suite with generous gravity and subtle recalls to Earth.

"I don't understand your madness," she'd said, after he'd told her what he wanted her to do. "I mean, has anything been diagnosed?"

He'd given her a thin smile, probably reserved for just these reactions. Sitting across from him, she'd leaned back and winced at her bluntness. "Sorry."

He understood his designs were demanding. "I know what I'm asking you to do, can it be *done*?"

She'd walked to the window, her dark dress contrasting with the stars beyond. Black leaves were woven into her silver hair. The latest fashion on Europa was, according to Karl, *nostalgia and guilt*. These remnants pervaded and contaminated everything; his views weren't unfamiliar to her.

Eventually she'd turned. "It can be done, but it's... vandalism."

He'd given her an even thinner smile. "I want to build a room that I can be alone in, entirely on my terms. That's all."

"But why *this*?"

That was the question he'd never answered.

Evie waited for him in his new office, dressed casual, before prepping for her suit. She tried not to think of the harsh technology around her, the walls buzzing, the shields dancing in their lurid quantum interactions. Her bare feet pressed into the cold floor, and she embraced the sensation. The feeling, so delicate, could so easily be lost.

Karl smiled as he entered the room. Not an old man, but his youth had left him. His hair was fading to silver when once it had been black as the space between stars. He still stood tall, lean. They exchanged a firm handshake. "It's everything I wanted," he said, looking around, "and more."

She handed him a document, a symbolic passing over. "Here it is," she said, "a home carved into a star. Now *that's* privacy," she allowed a tight smile.

A look he gave her told her he appreciated the scale of the achievement. "Thank you for this."

"Just a shame it's a tomb." When he didn't respond, she added, "What if you change your mind?"

"I want to be alone." His tone was clear and firm. Beyond this, there was no explanation owed.

She shook her head. They had no relationship beyond this contract, only really knew each other by their reputations, but as she walked past him she stopped. This had become far more than curiosity. She had glimpsed something in these walls, in his designs, something in *pain*.

"Please tell me why I built *this*? Why am I leaving you here?"

His expression became raw, as if he was struggling to evade thoughts that had unbearable depths. He looked at her until it seemed to hurt. "You're from one of the colonies?"

Evie nodded. "Trans-Neptunian."

He looked away, glancing at the paintings with something strangely wistful. Some of the landscapes weren't terran, but otherworldly skies framed in optimistic strokes. "Took my family out there," he said. "Wife, a daughter – she'd be your age now – went through the Heliopause, headed to the far colonies. I was going to help design the new sun..."

Her eyes widened.

To his design, the floors were black. He stared down at a reflection that haunted the marble. "They never made it," he said softly. "And I never wanted to make it alone. Now every person I meet out there is a ghost that reminds me of another ghost. Nothing is as real as what I lost. I want no part of it."

He looked around; whether he was moved, pained, or overwhelmed, she couldn't tell.

"But I was determined to build this. She wanted to live in the stars, I told her we could live *in* a star, and I never got to show her what I meant."

Evie understood that plans fell apart; she hadn't gone into space to carve up stars.

She gave the room a last extensive look, then gave him a final nod. "Okay."

Suiting up, Evie crossed the Lightbridge and watched her feet hover over eternity. Ahead, her crew were waiting on the *Artisan*. She thought of the moment when she'd punch in the numbers and kill the bridge forever. No one would be able to reconnect it, no one could summon it again.

She looked out and saw the black pulse of the stars beyond the barrier of the bridge, light engulfed in darkness engulfed in light. Endless. Like hurt.

Had he made a grave of his life, or carved away a piece of immortality, all in their name? Was this the only thing left to him that felt like peace?

She climbed into the *Artisan's* airlock, and waited for the decontamination to end. Stopping at the first terminal she found, she started to enter the signal. It felt wrong to linger, to dwell. There was no ceremony, but she paused before sending. She gave him a moment, a wish for his sanctuary to outshine his sorrow, then sealed off the star.

The monochromatic display flickered, and she saw the black lines of the interior structure fade. Like scars, that vanished with time.

Evie watched until it was all white, then turned and walked away.

Barry Charman is a writer living in North London. He has been published in various magazines, including *Ambit, Fireworks Quarterly, Mothership Zeta* and *Popshot.* He has had poems published online and in print, most recently in *Bewildering Stories* and The *Linnet's Wings.*
He has a blog at http://barrycharman.blogspot.co.uk

Goddess with a
Human Heart

Jeannette Ng

Art: Sara Julia

The speaker outside my window splutters to life. Between the static and the distorted, mechanical voice it is impossible to make out the time being announced.

But I know. I have three hours left.

My hand creeps unconsciously to my chest and rests on my beating, fluttering heart. Caged in bones and bound in flesh, it longs for something more. It has a fate apart from me. It aches.

I turn on my bunk to face the window and its cramped view of the street outside. I can see the edge of the ziggurat from here. It is early and the lights are beginning to spark. It is pretty, in a way.

I remember the first time I saw the Goddess in the temple. My legs and feet had been sore from climbing the great ziggurat. I had huddled at the top of steps, frowning at my shiny child shoes, their heels stained with machine oil. My doll of knotted rags was tucked under my arm. I chewed my braid as people streamed past me. I heard my mother call.

I had looked up and all those petty, pretty things fell away.

The Goddess who Listens to the Suffering of the World.

She was arranged cross-legged among and upon the endless tangle of wires and tubes and pipes that fed Her. They are Her thousand hands and thousand eyes. Above Her, shrouded in a thick haze of machine smoke, were the thick coils of Her thinking, blinking databanks. In days of old, She was depicted with a spread of arms behind her back, like the spokes of a great wheel. Each arm would end in a hand with an eye at the palm. Each would hold something different: a sword, a book, a fan, a branch, a reminder of all she could do. But now, we know Her true form.

I felt Her eyes on me and was suddenly aware of my own inconsequence as a child: all plump cheeks, stubby limbs and cute sharpened teeth.

I looked for Her face; it was under a crown of spiralling glass cables that feathered the light into a dizzying array of colour, obscuring most of her features. I could just about make out half-closed, sunken eyes and high, sharp cheekbones and the shadow of lips. Her cheeks were stained red with machine oil from her crown of cables. I imagined she looked upon us with infinite, ineffable wisdom.

Her real, mortal arms had long been severed and had been arranged like the petals of a lotus around Her torso. One of her hands held a tiny light that cast a red glow onto the papery, preserved skin of her arms. Her robes seemed to whisper gently with Her every breath. One of the folds had shifted from Her shoulder and I could see the rows of glinting medical staples down her left breast.

Three hours. Or rather, a little less now.

I am older now, but part of me will always remain that awe-struck little girl. It is that little girl's heart that the Goddess needs in Her. The priests have counted the days and it is time. We owe it to Her. And we need Her.

I curl into myself. The priests will be here for me soon. My eyes fall on the pale green robe that hangs in wait for me. I shudder; clutch the sheets closer to myself. My stomach clenches and the urge to hurl pulses at the back of my throat. I try to breathe.

Again and again, my mind returns to the stories of the past, of how the gods and goddesses walked among us. Always at the end of the tale, the deities would cast off the mortal skins they wore and revealed themselves to their followers.

Ages rise and fall. Each age begins with blood and ends with blood, for that is how the days are measured. The people are transformed and a new sun rises from the ashes.

The bright sun of the fifth age, Left-Handed Hummingbird, was slain by his sister the moon, She whose Face is Painted with Bells. She led the stars in a war against him and we nourished our sun with sacrifices of blood and bone. We called ourselves the People of the Sun. For a while, it seemed enough.

Until, of course, one day, when it wasn't. Our brave, proud warrior sun was poisoned by his treacherous sister. It darkened and cooled and we gave up more and more of ourselves to feed him. The war of the heavens continued, and as Left-Handed Hummingbird dimmed, we knew it was the end of the fifth age and we knew our deaths to be written. It is the way of the world, that each age end in blood and fire.

That was when the Goddess appeared.

From beyond the darkness, She found us. She heard our suffering. She was the reflection that hid in the obsidian mirror of our pantheon. She snaked from its ink-black surface like smoke and promised us life. She saved us from the darkness and became our new sun.

We built our new world around Her, though we gave it an old name: Aztlán. Enthroned in Her temple atop the greatest ziggurat ever built by mortal hands, She sits at the heart of our metropolis. She hears our suffering, shapes our world and illuminates our darkness. Her databanks arrange and organise every aspect of our great metropolis, from the times of the cloudrail to every suncoil that shines on every waterfield.

I swallow, though my mouth is still dry and my stomach unsettled. I try not to think of all the things I will leave unfinished in my room. Scrap-rag serials I will never know the endings of. That scrap of knitting I will never finish. The milk that will expire after I breathe my last. I should be finishing things, not turning over and over in my bunk. I want to pace, but there isn't the space in my cramped room.

The heart that beats in me is not my own. It belongs to the Goddess and it has always belonged to Her. I am not a sacrifice; I am merely a vessel for Her heart, a mortal skin that She needs to shed.

I imagine the obsidian scalpel against my breast, and my stomach knots. This mortal skin has felt too much already. We are meant to surrender Her heart to Her when it is still unburdened by such feelings.

Perhaps I am already too old for this.

It has been said that as the days are counted, the human heart within the Goddess hardens to the sounds of our suffering. With each beat, it turns Her away from us. Humans, after all, are not made for boundless mercy. We are small, petty creatures, finite in our loves and likes.

And so she needs a new heart every three years. Before they break.

In the last count of days and years, heretics have disrupted the transplanting of the Goddess' heart. The blessed hour passed and the black scalpel did not fall. Last time, I sat in this room wide-eyed and full of hope. I remember sitting on the edge of my bed, feet dangling impatiently as I waited for Father Itztli. I was fearless, then, and I knew only love. I wanted only to surrender to the Goddess what was Hers by right.

It has since been three long years.

With shaking hands, I undress. I resist the urge to study the dark, gangly shape in my mirror as I reach for the robe. Vanity will do me no good now. The synthetic is crisp against my skin. The back ties are awkward, but I manage. There is no need to be neat. I bind my old running shoes to my feet. I try not to think of how this will be the last time I wear them.

The yellow streetlights flicker and I glance out. Hunched figures in white and red shuffle down the street. I watch the steel door slide open and the three shapes disappear through. I can smell the pungent mix of incense and machine oil before I can hear their footsteps.

They are here.

The door gives a beep before it opens. Father Itztli steps in, followed by two other priests. They smile at me, bowing their heads gravely and gesturing me peace.

"Are you ready, little one?" says Itztli. He is beautiful, as all priests are. His hair falls in a mass of turquoise and garnet augments.

I bite my tongue. Desire coils and uncoils around the heart that isn't mine. Irrationally, I want to hear my name from his lips, but I know he cannot bring himself to say it.

"Are you ready?" he repeats.

"As ready as the sun is to set at dusk." My voice sounds hollow and the ritualised words devoid of meaning. I remember the hours I have spent meditating upon them, for they would be my last. It is strange to speak of these things in terms of ancient celestial phenomena. "Thank you, Itztli."

For a moment, he hesitates. He licks his lips and very slowly, he swallows. "Give us a moment."

"But —" says one of the priests.

"We are five minutes ahead. It will be fine."

The two priests exchange unreadable looks and leave us. As the door glides shut behind them, I find myself shaking. I am breathing heavily.

"Yoltzin," he begins, but I throw myself at him, winding my arms tightly around him. His breath catches. My fingers tangle into his robes and the heart that isn't mine aches.

I know this heart loves him because he is Her high priest. And I know I love him for shallow reasons: because he has dark eyes, because his hair is beautiful, because his voice is soft and enchanting. It changes nothing.

We stay like this for long moments, him rigid and still in my arms, me clutching desperately at him. The knotted cord of his body tightens under my touch. He has balled his hands into fists. He dares not touch me.

But he breathes my name again and I am gasping, choking on dry sobs. I press my face against his stiff linen tunic. The strings of turquoise around his neck dig into me.

I feel as though I am drowning. I remember the, polluted waters of the Culiacán engulfing me as I plunged into them. It was Itztli, still an acolyte then, who was drowning and I rescued him. I dragged him from the dark waters of the canal. As he choked water from his lungs, he uttered Her divine name. Over and over in his delirium, he called out to Her. I did not know what to do, but I studied the sharp angles of his face and stroked the damp curls of his hair. I wanted to press my lips to his and kiss the name of the Goddess on them. I imagined it to be a sacrament; I understood so very little of the flesh.

My rescue of him was how they recognised me as the Goddess' vessel. I cling to him now as he did to me then.

The door beeps. I step from him and try to compose myself. The door opens.

They drape a heavy jacket over my shoulders and we leave. The streets are cold at this hour and the drains are steaming. The sky is a sickly yellow. A haze clings to the city like dust on windows. Aztlán is beginning to stir. The sight of people fumbling with their keys, walking from their homes, waiting for the skyrail all remind me how selfish I have been in my thoughts of Itztli.

The speakers choke out incoherent sounds. Two hours.

I have lived for long enough. Far longer than most vessels. I have had a room of my own, an unimaginable luxury. I shared one with siblings for most of my childhood. We used to fight each other for the crackling, foil-lined blankets, tumbling over and over in the dark.

We wind our way through the bleakness and into the ziggurat. Itztli casts a glance behind but his eyes do not settle on me. The steel doors close behind us. The air is suddenly heavier and warmer. It presses damp against my skin. I feel a low hum in my bones.

I shed my shoes and the jacket; acolytes take them from me. I briefly wonder if they will clothe another of the Goddess' vessels. The metal floor is warm against my bare feet. I am led to a steel operating table. For a moment, everything feels too still. I want to bolt, but I think again of the Goddess, of the city's peopled streets, of Itztli, and I calm myself. I lie down, stiffly.

A priest in a turquoise mask approaches. A shock of glass cables and feathers frame the fragmented shapes of the mosaic face. I know it to be Itztli. With gloved hands, Itztli presses the laryngeal mask to my face. I breathe deeply from it.

Before the blackness claims me, I see Itztli dip his head to kiss the mask.

\#

Light.

Warm, brilliant light washes over me in waves. I am in endless fields of light, each arcing beam a stalk, refracting into rainbows. I find myself wandering through the light, hands flitting through its feathery fronds. An indistinct lullaby from my childhood threads its way through the breeze.

The Goddess is crying.

She is a small child, curled like a sea-slug shell in a sobbing heap. Her hair sprawls out in a web, all sharp angles like the etchings on a circuit board, or the lines on a map of the thirteen heavens. She looks up at me with eyes that seem to have seen all of time. She reaches out to me with a thousand hands. She is looking at me and through me.

It suddenly seems so foolish to think that a change of mortal hearts every few years can fool a Goddess who Listens to the Suffering of the World. Tears stream from her face like light, like music, like waves. She hears every sorrow and feels the pain of this imperfect, created world. She cries because she cannot save us all.

I am wearing a garland of red flowers. I take it bleeding from my neck and drape it around hers. The Goddess smiles and closes Her eyes. The flowers bleed and bleed. Dark bruises blossom under her skin.

She crumples, still smiling with mottled skin, lying in a pool of infinite red.

✳

My eyes open.

I did not expect that. There is an aching, empty numbness across my chest. I try to sit up, but I seem to have no control over my limbs. A draught ghosts over my skin and I shiver. Bright colours dance at the edge of my vision.

"Don't move." It is Itztli's voice, gentle and firm. My head cannot turn to see him. "I'll prop you up."

My hand flies to my chest, or rather, tries to. My shoulder twitches and my left arm flails. Half my chest feels numb, though I can make out something heavily thudding inside me. Thoughts stumble and stagger in my clouded brain.

"What... my heart... the Goddess..."

He laughs, a sound I never thought to hear again. "Your heart of flesh and blood is in Her. Whatever good that does Her now." As he moves into view, I see him as though for the first time. His hair has been crudely shorn close to the scalp; he looks different without the shock of beads and wire augments. His shadowed eyes seem smaller without the dark lines. I notice again the sharp angles of his face, the sharp arch of his brow, the length of his lashes. The numbness in my chest deepens.

"She needs a heart," I murmur. I do not know if he can hear me.

Itztli arranges me into a sitting position. He is gentle, but it matters not. I can barely feel his touch. We are in a narrow corridor, dark but for a flicking light some paces ahead. Cables and pipes run the length of the walls and there is a low, persistent humming. There are numbers and markings, but they mean nothing to me.

"Why, when Her mind is stored in coiled databanks, does She need a human heart?" asks Itztli. "Why when they can make Her blinking wire-framed eyes and pulsing plastic innards can they not make Her a heart? It is nonsensical."

"But it is Her heart." The colours at the edge of my vision threatened to overwhelm me, flitting brilliance across my eyes.

He shakes his head. "That doesn't matter now. She won't survive it. I've..." There is an alien note of bitterness in his voice. "Don't you want to know how I saved you?"

"I'm supposed to be..." I grit my teeth; I did not want to use the word.

"I've put a part of Her in you." He glances down the corridor. "It's not exactly Her heart, but there really isn't much more to a heart than a series of valves and pumps. So it wasn't hard to adapt. There was so much blood. I was scared... After I took out yours –"

"It is not mine. It is Hers," I insist, though my voice sounds hollow, like an echo. It is strange to think that there is a part of the divine machine inside me. He says nothing and the silence is heavy between us. Though my mouth is dry, I swallow. "Why did..."

I try to pull myself to my feet, but cannot.

"You'll need to be carried," he says and folds me into his arms. I do not protest. I lean heavily against him. He smells of disinfectant, blood and beeswax. "Neither of us can go back. Because of what..." He does not finish the thought; he can no more speak of it than I can.

"I don't... I... why?" I force breath into my restricted lungs. "Why did you do that?"

"You saved me. That matters."

"The Goddess saved you."

"No." His voice is a whisper, but firm. I can feel him swallow. "She damned me. And you. It doesn't matter now. It is all sophistry."

"Of course it matters. It's the Goddess. She sees everything."

He gives a brief, bitter scoff of a laugh.

"She does. She listens to our suffering. She knows you. Her heart loved you because She saw your suffering. She understands." The pain that was vague and distant before is beginning to coalesce into a heavy, thudding knot in my chest. "She knows you did whatever you did. She knows we are down here. She allows it."

Pain devours up the numbness inside me; the shock is almost electric. I choke out a cry.

"The anaesthetics are probably... don't move. Just don't move." He swallows, trying to calm himself. "It'll be fine. It'll be fine." He slurs the words as though they were a litany. Fleetingly, he seems again that priest who taught me how to read, how to pray and how to drag a rope of thorns through my tongue.

My eyes flutter shut, but through the angry, mechanical rhythm of the thing inside me, I hear the clink of glass and metal. I hear the needle and syringe rather than feel it. Raw, wild colours roar through my vision before subsiding again into the black behind my eyelids.

When I reopen my eyes, the shapes in the dark seem sharper and cold, more keen.

"She hears us. Every day." I mouth to Itztli. "If She allowed this. Then this is. This is Her plan."

He closes his eyes. His face contorts; more emotion than I have ever seen him show in our years together. "We should keep moving."

I say nothing and he carries me down the corridors. I imagine we are in the disused underbelly of the ziggurat, but I do not do so with certainty. Itztli picks his way through increasingly twisted passages.

The outside is nothing more than shadows and shapes at the edge of my blurring vision. Itztli presses me close to his chest. I can hear his heart beat against me now. It is a closeness that I had previously hungered for.

The street corner speakers declare the hour. I guess it to be late given the colour of the lights. Judging from the quality of the speakers, we are in a rough quadrant of the city. I allow my eyes to drift shut and the pain to claim me. If I think only of the pain, concentrate on its myriad shades stretching and clenching inside me, I can keep from crying out. It hurts more when he sprints, but thankfully he does not do that often.

Itztli pauses several times before continuing. Each time, I hear his voice through the haze: "It'll be fine. It'll be fine."

Leaning on an archaic door to open it, we enter into a building. Voices greet him. Frantic, heartfelt concern melts into indistinct congratulations and curiosity.

"Is that it? That why you joined us?"

"I thought she'd be –"

"It's not as though the Goddess Herself is a looker."

That got a laugh from the others, though I can feel Itztli's grip on me tighten at the blasphemy. He sits but he does not put me down. I feel a wall against my back, but his arms are still around me.

The voices around us plan and plot. I follow more the cadence of the voices than the substance of their plans. There will be a new world and a new age, one without light and without a sun, watched over by no God.

※

Days pass. I am bundled in the corner of the room, half-forgotten by most of the heretics. Itztli has been playing surgeon for them and he tends to me. I remember little but for a certain warmth of arms, a constant constricting pain and thin soup against my lips. I remember choking on blood and vomit. I remember needles and colours too bright to be real.

I also remember this:

"Are you awake?" Itztli whispers against my ear. I am still. I try to speak, but my throat contracts. The beat of the thing inside my chest feels odd and alien.

Distantly, I can feel fingertips following the angles of my face, stroking my hair, the line of my lips. "I'm sorry. I'm sorry I never told you, Yoltzin. But until I did what needed to be done, we could not speak the plan aloud. I know you believed. But She... The count of days is wrong. We are not the sixth age. We are but the death throes of the fifth. We are part of the catastrophe of the age's end. We are not living in a new and glorious age, we are merely the last of a dying one, needlessly dragging out the pain of our people. I am just ending what needs to be ended. I am just saving you."

Every word of his is heresy. I try to force open my eyes, but I do not have the strength. I breathe in shallow, swift gasps. I manage a low whimper of pain, but not words. The journey has been more taxing than either of us anticipated.

"The others will build a new world without the need for endless sacrifice. There will be no part in it for a priest old before his time, a priest with this much blood on his hands. There will be no part in it for an old sacrifice either, an old sacrifice who still believes. But I had to. I had to save you. I just…

"I killed the Goddess. I won't be able to tell you when you wake, but I need to say this now. I killed Her. I slipped a knife into Her heart when I stapled shut Her chest. She will bleed."

At the mention of blood, my mind turns to the red flowers and the blossoming bruises on the Goddess. In more ancient times, they called such human sacrifice a flowery death. It was said to be the most noble way to die. I remember the pictures we were shown as children, the men and women sprawled out in bright blossoms of blood, each splatter uncurling like a petal from their heart.

"She will bleed under Her skin," whispers Itztli. "The blood will clog the parts that are inside Her. She will lose too much. She will die before they notice."

"She…" The immensity of the realisation pushes me to form words. I croak them out despite the pain. "She wanted you to…"

Itztli recoils.

"She wanted you to. I saw Her. She showed me." I keep my eyes closed, but I fumble a hand towards Itztli. I stroke a finger down his jaw. His skin is cold, too cold. Instead of the suncoils and the skyrail, my mind returns to the smile I saw in my dream of light. It dawns on me, colours unravelling endlessly in my mind like all the sunrises I have only ever imagined, pressing grubby fingers on yellowing picbook pages. "She hears everything. She hears everyone. Even those who fight against her priests and her enforcers. She can only bear our sorrows and suffering for so long. She wanted you to end it. She wanted a new age."

"No." His voice is thick and warm against my ear. "This is not yours to forgive."

"There is nothing to forgive."

He does not believe me, but he holds me tighter, probably too tight. It barely matters through the drugs and the pain.

I try to focus on the way he and I fit together: my head on his shoulder, the tangle of his hands, the twinning hold of his legs. I want to think only on the way his cold skin and the knot of his scars feel against me. I want desperately for this to be the only thing that matters. He has torn out most of his augments and he smells of old blood and sweat. I wonder if he sought to flay off his skin this way, in a penance of sorts. He does not carry his crime lightly.

Pain cuts through these thoughts and the erratic beat of the mechanical heart consumes me; I hear it echo in my ears.

I cannot forget.

※

Look above, child.

The sun you see today is not the sun that shone above the first people. Five ages and five tyrant suns have risen and fallen. Ours will one day fall as well.

The first was the Lord of Near and Nigh. But his brother, the Feathered Serpent, was envious of how the once crippled god shone, so he knocked him from of the firmament with a stone club. Without the sun, the people were lost to darkness and in that darkness they turned on one another. They consumed each other and in their barbarism, they became jaguars.

The next age was ruled by the Feathered Serpent. He died in wind and rage, with its people clinging to trees and becoming monkeys.

He Who Is Made of Earth ascended as the next sun but his wife was kidnapped and thus he wallowed in narcissistic grief. Besieged by prayers, he destroyed the world in a rain of fire. To escape, the people became birds, soaring above the flaming sea.

The fourth age ended with its people becoming fish as the goddess had a heart too soft, too kind and too broken. She flooded the world with her black tears. A man and woman survived, hiding in a hollow tree, but found themselves being turned into dogs by the gods. We do not live in a time of just gods.

The fifth sun, Left-Handed Hummingbird, demanded unending sacrifice of hearts upon his altars of blood and bone. But the moon, She whose Face is Painted with Bells, knew this to be unjust, so she made war upon him night after night. But war

was a stalemate and unable to witness the suffering of the people, she poisoned her own brother.

Then came the time of blood and burning. We have lived in the shadow of the fifth age, in its final breaths. As with the end of every age, the trials made us into beasts as we cling to survival. The Goddess with the Human Heart could not bear the suffering any longer and the Last Priest killed her in an act of mercy, ending the time of sacrifice.

And so dawned a sixth age. There is a new sun and a new people, but tyrants do not live forever. I hear the Last Priest and the Girl with the Divine Heart wander the wastes. I hear they are near.

The wheel of the heavens will turn again.

Jeannette Ng was born in Hong Kong and now lives in Durham. She designs and plays live roleplaying games, makes costumes and writes speculative fiction. Her debut novel *Under The Pendulum Sun* is published in October 2017 by Angry Robot.

These Are the Ways

Premee Mohamed

These are the ways I wished for you to die:

Fighting, to assure your family of honour.
With courage, for the comfort of your immortal soul.
Swiftly, that you might not suffer at the end.
And at my side.

The plasma arc hit low, scorching calf and flank, and at first we thought it was not fatal, not even serious; we'd all seen burns like that in training, same shape, same size. You joked as we pulled off your melted boot and snipped away the damaged remains of your uniform trousers. "Hey guys, do I need to shave this week?"

"Smooth as a baby's butt," Kara said, setting aside the scissors and cracking open her damaged first-aid box. Medics and their black humour. As a sniper, I was useless except as extra hands for the hurried field dressing. I held your ankle on my shoulder, encircling the knobbly warmth with my entire hand, your eyes meeting mine accusingly between frantic blinks that barely cleared the pain-sweat. I should not even have been there, your eyes told me. That was the rule. Useful personnel: continue the assault. The wounded ("We do not say 'hurt'," the major had snapped): repaired and sent back into action if possible; gathered and guarded if not, to prevent the Akhjians from taking POWs. As a last resort, gassed.

Kara worked quickly – anaesthetic aerosol, antibiotic gel, a lint-free paper sleeve, pressure dressing, a blast of UV to harden the resin enough to bear weight. Someone had sent one of the privates, big Gilmour, to fetch you a new boot. Wounded himself, he gamely zigzagged across the battlefield between pops of green and violet light, looking for a size 7.

"This is bad," murmured the other medic, stiffly rising and shutting his kit. "Maybe we should—"

"I'm fine," you snapped. "Gimme a couple of pain pills for later and let's just get this push over with."

"I agree," Kara said, gesturing at me to lower your leg. "Thanks for helping, Jen. I know you don't like blood. Can you wait with her till Gilly comes back? X'eo and I have to keep moving."

"Of course," I said, and placed your foot in my lap as they trotted off, keeping low. In the dust and darkness soon all that was visible was the reflective cross on the back of their jackets. The ground rumbled ominously. That wasn't small-arms fire, let alone the broad-spray plasma arcs on either side. What else did the aliens have that our intelligence hadn't told us about?

In the blood and antiseptic-soaked mud you squirmed for your gun, fingers running across the grimy plastic, automatically checking load and range with the feedback dots. "Oof. How's it look?"

"Messy," I said, "but shallow. I think Patra got a worse one in training last year, and she was fine."

"Ugly, but fine."

"She was ugly before."

"Ugly like me," you said, and laughed faintly. But you weren't ugly, you were just you, touchy about the smallness and lightness that I loved, a little wild animal in baggy fatigues, running faster, packing more, shooting straighter than anyone else to prove that a girl from Crutas, of all planets, could make it in the corps. To prove that someone whose nickname ranged between 'Cockroach' and 'Mousie' could win a war.

"Does it hurt?" I asked.

"Burns some. I think they're running out of deadspray."

"Could be."

"Why's the ground shaking like that, Jen? It's not an earthquake. And it doesn't feel like ground troops..."

"I don't know. I hate to imagine."

"Well, I'm glad you can feel it too. Thought maybe it was just me." In the dark, I saw your dark eyes crinkle in amusement, moistly ringed with salt. Gilmour returned with a dirty but unbloodied boot, the nanoceramic tan rather than black. Just as I opened my mouth to rib him about it, the ground heaved rather than trembled, and he fell to his knees in the mud.

"Time to jet," you said. "Jen, do you mind?"

"You owe me for this degradation." I tugged the boot over your bare foot, ignoring your hiss of pain, laced it tightly, made sure to tuck in the bandage on your calf. "Private Gilmour, please assist Corporal Nemerin to verticality and draw your service weapon; we will be moving as a three-person unit until cessation of original orders."

"Yes, ma'am."

He easily got you upright, and we disentangled, moving into the darkness along the battle lines planned the day before. Your pulse-rifle; my plasma arc and a dozen grenades; Gilly's laser pistol and extra cells. We were a walking bomb; if anyone shot us, our drop ship would see the explosion from low orbit. I wondered what it would look like: lightning under clouds, maybe, but what colour?

I wanted to reach out as we stumbled in that nightmare landscape, the ground bucking under our boots, to put a hand under your elbow and feel the warmth of those light bones. Not to support you – you and your pride both would have been a heavy burden – just to touch you for a moment. But Gilly planted himself between us with some half-invented idea of chivalry and ploughed ahead, helmet swivelling like clockwork. Something rose from the rocks ahead of us, invisible except for the glint off its goggles; I drew smoothly and fired at the fleck of light, watched it disintegrate into green chunks.

"Very nice," you grunted. "Have you been practicing in secret? We'll have to have a re-match when we get back."

"No thanks; I'm already a month behind in pay thanks to you."

We slowed; I glanced at Gilmour in case he had seen anything, but it was you, limping heavily, the chrysanthemum odour of your sweat overpowering the smell of the antibiotic gel. As one, we looked down; an obliging flash a hundred yards away lit up your bare leg, no longer the sterile white of the bandage but soaking red, flowing easily over the cuff of your new boot, washing it clean of mud. Gilmour yelped. I held back a noise of my own. And you, you, my love...

"I'm fine. Come on."

We destroyed a scouting party, walked through their stinking remains, caught ourselves constantly on a knee or an outstretched hand as the ground shuddered. Gilmour came within an inch of stepping into a steam-vent that opened under his boot; you yanked him back, and we stood abruptly marooned in a ring of blood, dust, steam, and glowering cracks. Expressions emerged in the dim, orange light. You looked resigned, Gilly baldly terrified.

Despite the comms ban, we heard a crackle from our sternum radios – a shock, hearing the voice of the ship after so many days. "Attention all personnel in quadrant C. The Akhjians have activated a seismic weapon in this vicinity. Do not engage further. Return to muster point Romeo, repeat, Romeo, and await pickup. You have. Seven. Minutes. And. Forty-five. Seconds."

"How far is it?" I whispered.

You said, "Half a mile. Come on."

I trusted your sense of direction; mine was pathetic, and Gilmour had an extremely good one that was unfortunately ninety degrees out of true on this planet. Yours was the only one I would have followed. And so we did, weaving through gaps in the vents, panting at the noxious gases they spat out. I fumbled absently for my rebreather, lost hours ago; yours was filled with blood. Gilly handed you his at once, and I hope he saw the look I gave him in the volcanic twilight.

The ship itself could not be seen, but we looked up and saw its green lights hanging against the faint silver stars still visible through the clouds of dust and steam. I cried out at its nearness.

"Corporal," Gilly called. "Please—"

I looked back and saw that I had been walking alone; you had gone down, the saturated bandage finally peeling away to reveal the arc burn no less ravaged than the land around us, bubbling with blood and lymph. I dropped beside you. The mud was so hot I felt my skin scald at once.

"Get up," I told you.

"I can't."

"Can't, or won't?" I snapped, quoting the major. A smile flickered across your face, quick and dark. Your eyes were like the sky hidden above us.

"Give me your grenades. I'll give those bastards a sendoff to remember."

"We'll carry you," I said. "Gilmour."

"Ma'am." He reached down for you and reeled back, lip split, landing heavily on his back. I would not have thought your small fist could have carried so much force. You were licking your knuckles, face set and drawn.

"I'm not going to make it, Jen," you said, voice miles away. As if in agreement, a six-foot crack opened up nearly at our feet, white inside rather than red, a sudden jerk of earth skywards.

"Corporal!" shouted Gilly; we heard another number, incomprehensible, through the radio. I ignored it.

"You can. You will. Look how close we are."

You slid a hand into my jacket, the familiar coolness of your nimble fingers, and just as I was about to touch your face I saw that you had taken my plasma arc and gently pressed the barrel to my throat. I felt my blood tick against it, pulse metronoming out of the corner of my eye. "Unhook your grenades and give them to me," you said softly. "And then run, my love."

It was the first time you'd said it. Something exploded nearby, showered us with pattering grit, shook the tears from my cheeks. Your eyes were dry. You wanted to die not merely with honour, but in the carnage of any enemy foolish enough to approach you. I unclipped the belt and dropped it into your lap, hearing the end splash into a widening pool of blood. Your free hand met my hair, tangled in the curls, then fell away. "What medal do you want?" I whispered.

"The biggest one they've got, of course."

One swift kiss, tasting of dirt and sulphur, and then I was running, supporting Gilmour, counting down as the ship hovered, swayed, dropped below the cloud cover. Acid burned in my throat. The mud was a treadmill, we grew no closer, and the land itself fought progress, throwing up slabs and boulders and sinkholes filled with boiling mud. We vaulted vents, wrenched ankles on the far side, burned our palms. The ship's ramp was still down, only beginning to retract as we approached.

"No!" Gilmour cried.

I snatched his pistol from its holster and fired into the air, one, two, three, and watched through a glaze of fresh tears as the ramp paused. And then we slid into the circle of its light, strange hands pulling us up, dumping us into a pile of uniforms and warm limbs and clean air. I pressed my face to the floor and tried not to vomit.

Someone hauled me up by my jacket: Kara the medic. "My God, Jen! You're alive! Is Thea coming?"

But I dragged myself to the viewport as we teetered into the air, grasping a grab-rail – yes, there. An Akhjian ship arrowed into the darkness and went up without warning in a string of turquoise fireballs, the micro-stellar cores of the grenades, flickering the lights on our ship.

"No," I said when it was over. "She got what she wanted."

That's what they say on Crutas, I know; you had told me one night, late, jigsawed together on my bunk, eating each other's whispers. There are bad deaths, easily known, and there are good deaths, which are subtle, which can only be judged as a piece of the whole.

And you died the way you wished. A good death.

Premee Mohamed is an Indo-Caribbean scientist and spec fic writer based in Alberta, Canada. Her work has been published by Nightmare Magazine, Martian Migraine Press, Innsmouth Free Press, and many others. She can be found on Twitter at @premeesaurus.

Arthur Kovic's Days of Change

Michael Teasdale

Art: Becca McCall

Friday

It is evening on a day like any other.

Children are tired and exhausted. Adults, glad of the temporary reprieve, snooze peacefully in front of chattering television sets and poke at their TV dinners. On the flickering tubes, game show hosts crack lame jokes about mother-in-laws and the streets outside lie empty. The crickets are singing their evening lullabies and the encroaching dusk paints the sky a lurid shade of orange.

All is calm.

Arthur Kovic enjoys the sunset. He admires it for its quiet regularity and the way it always arrives, like a familiar friend, to usher in an end to the daily madness of meetings, appointments and complex office politics.

The weekend is here and Arthur smiles. Tomorrow will be his birthday and Anna is planning a surprise party.

He has practiced his planned expression several times in front of the bathroom mirror. "Oh, how wonderful," he will say. Then he will raise his eyebrows in a carefully rehearsed display of dazzled duplicity.

Arthur Kovic likes to be prepared. He does not enjoy surprises or situations that require him to ad-lib, which is why Anna is always careful to warn him in advance.

As he reverses up the drive, he switches off the car radio to better enjoy the satisfying crunch of his premium gravel.

It is important to find pleasure in the small things in life.

Arthur read this in a book. The author of the book is a successful man. Arthur wants, very much, to be a successful man.

"Evening, Neighbour."

Ned stands by his lawnmower on the other side of the garden fence. In one hand he clutches a can of *Pab's Blue Ribbon*, as he strokes his greying beard.

"Good evening, Ned," says Arthur.

They nod quietly at one another. All the wisdom that the world needs at 7:00pm on a Friday evening is communicated in the reassuring familiarity of such gestures.

It is the small things that keep the world turning, thinks Arthur, *the everyday normalities that give us strength.*

Arthur unlocks the door and slips off his loafers, wiggling his toes and allowing them to breathe through the cloying cotton of his thick, black socks. The big toe of his left foot waves up at him through a newly punctured hole. It is a familiar problem. No matter how frequently he clips his toenails, the toes do not want to stay hidden from view, poking through like ugly, alien rebels.

Arthur does not like his toes.

He pads through to the kitchen where the scent of boiling vegetables is causing his stomach to knot with hunger. The limp sandwich he had for lunch has done nothing to abate it.

His interest in Anna's cooking is so all consuming that, as he enters the kitchen, he almost fails to notice the girl sitting at the kitchen table.

The girl is not his daughter Jennifer. She has a set of raven coloured pigtails that trail down the shoulders of a grass stained t-shirt. Jennifer's pigtails are a mousy blonde. Below her gingham skirt, the girl is barefoot and her pale, thin legs swing nonchalantly back and forth like the ticking pendulums of an erratic grandfather clock. She does not look at Arthur as he enters the kitchen. Instead she stares in fixed concentration at the large sheet of cartridge paper she has laid out in front of her. With a worn-down colouring pencil, she scribbles furiously as her protruding tongue hops from one side of her mouth to the other. A sea of stationary lies scattered across the table. There is no sign of Jennifer and yet her friend seems either unaware or unconcerned by Arthur's presence as he stands, momentarily transfixed by the rhythmic swinging of the girl's milky legs.

In the end it is only the sudden hissing of the saucepan, as it begins to bubble over and singe on the heat of the electric hob, which causes him to break away from the girl's hypnotic motion.

Arthur hurries over to the hob and removes the lid; watching as the overflowing bubbles begin to dissipate and a collection of wiggling green beans glare accusingly up at him from beneath the foam.

He feels himself blushing for a reason he cannot fully explain as he re-covers the vegetables, turning down the heat and placing the saucepan back on the hob.

Despite his commotion, the girl has not looked up from her drawing and Arthur wanders over to the table to see what she is doing.

"Hello," he says, "that's a nice picture."

The girl does not answer him. Instead she continues scribbling, furiously; adorning the wings of a large, ornately detailed butterfly.

After a few seconds she puts down the pencil.

"There's a hole in your sock," she announces.

Arthur looks down at the protruding big toe. He feels quietly ashamed.

The girl begins to slide herself down from the stool.

"It's silly to be scared of butterflies," she scolds him and then pokes out her tongue in a wry act of childish rebellion.

Arthur does not know how to respond to either the gesture or the accusation and so he reverts to a childish mentality himself, poking out his own tongue in response.

The girl laughs. Arthur does not like the laugh. There are secrets in a laugh like this one. Arthur does not like secrets any more than he likes toes.

"I'm going outside to play with Rachel," announces the girl and she skips past him, and out through the lobby. "See you later," she calls, as she disappears into the garden, slamming the front door behind her.

Arthur stands alone in the kitchen. On the table top, the half completed picture of the butterfly flaps briefly at the closing of the front door, before settling into stillness. The only sound now is the dull roar of the stove's solitary flame and the green beans bubbling quietly.

"But… I am *not* afraid of butterflies," says Arthur Kovic.

He says the words out loud.

He wonders why he did.

✳

"Who was the girl downstairs? A friend of Jennifer's? I've never seen her before."

Arthur Kovic stands by the wardrobe. He is wearing grey boxer shorts and the dishevelled upper remnants of his work clothes. He has removed the sock with the hole and thrown it away, although he is still wearing the other. Carefully he undoes his tie and slips it over the hanger.

"Mmm…" moans Anna from beneath the crumpled duvet.

His wife of fifteen years lies crippled by a migraine. She has forgotten the pot that she set boiling. It is not the first time.

Arthur describes the dark-haired girl to Anna as he hangs up his trousers, neatly folding out the creases, and finally removing the useless, leftover sock. He sits down on the edge of the bed and feels Anna shift away from him as he does so.

He opens his mouth to ask where Jennifer is this evening but quickly thinks better of it. His wife can offer no logical explanation. Anna can offer nothing at all when the migraines come.

Arthur sits for a moment, looking at the smooth white island of her shoulder blade, protruding from beneath the duvet. After a moment he stands up and heads, wordlessly, to the shower.

✳

With the bathroom door locked and the warm waters cascading down on him, Arthur masturbates in the shower. He does not think about anything much at all as he does so.

When he is finished, he sits quietly on the edge of the bathtub and applies fungal foot powder. The masturbation and the foot powder have become part of a weekend ritual. They help to make the unpleasant itching between his toes and in his brain dissipate. He cannot remember the last time he and Anna had sex. Arthur remembers that tomorrow is his birthday and quietly begins to dread the possibility that Anna may feel compelled to remedy this. Arthur looks down at his feet and the flaccid penis that sits dripping onto the tiles of the bathroom floor. He looks at his face, reflected back in the misted bathroom mirror. It looks the same as it ever did.

Outside the birds are singing and Arthur smiles. It is a nice evening. He will go out into the greenhouse before dinner and attend to his tomatoes.

※

In the greenhouse, Arthur waters the plants and listens to the dulcet tones of a radio program on soil erosion. Arthur has built the greenhouse himself and he is proud that everything inside of it is something he made live. Every year he repeats the same process: Six to eight weeks before the last of the spring frost occurs, he plants the seeds. He transplants them just as the soil has begun to warm. He enjoys carving the stakes and watching the slow, familiar process of the shoots as they curl around the posts.

This year should be a good crop, thinks Arthur and he tips the watering can and watches the little pots of earth slowly begin to moisten.

As he puts down the watering can, he notices something hanging by a thread from the greenhouse door. Arthur Kovic knows every inch of his greenhouse and can spot something out of place in a second.

The last of the natural light is fading and so he switches on the greenhouse lamp and wanders over to inspect the new thing. It is small, about two inches in length and an inch in diameter, with hard ridges lining its upper surface: A tiny chrysalis.

Arthur stands in silence, staring at the chrysalis, as if he is expecting something to happen. Then he goes inside to attend to supper.

✳

Arthur Kovic dreams: strange and formless dreams. In the dreams there is a heart beating, but Arthur does not think it is his own. In the dreams it is not entirely dark but the world is, instead, dimly illuminated by a soft, brown light. Things move and shift in the lugubrious, auburn embers of the dream. Things that, at first, appear to be a familiar blend and morph into things that slowly creep into the strange. The dream things frighten him. Arthur tries to speak, but the shape of his mouth does not feel entirely the same anymore and the words that come out are distorted and wrong.

Everything is wrong in the dream.

He feels he is on the verge of discovering a terrible secret and is overcome with the belief that, when he does, it will somehow all be his fault.

He wakes up, in a cold sweat, to the sound of music.

Saturday

The music fills him with tranquillity. A soft piano accompanies the voice of Nina Simone as it drifts up the staircase and floods him with a reassuring calm. He turns over to the empty space where Anna lay. The migraines did not abate throughout the night and he had expected that today would bring much of the same: that it would be a good excuse for her to cancel the planned festivities. He is surprised, therefore, to find the mattress lying empty before him, the curtains partially drawn and the sunlight filtering in across the hardwood floor.

Arthur smiles as he sits up.

From the kitchen downstairs the delicious aroma of frying bacon drifts into his nostrils as he yawns and stretches. Shrugging off the disturbing dreams of the night before, he stands up and reaches for his dressing gown.

Arthur sits at the dining table chewing over a mouthful of bacon dipped in the yolk of a lightly poached egg.

The breakfast surprised him almost as much as the unexpected kiss he received upon entering the kitchen. He tries to remember the last time Anna kissed him. *Perhaps she is practising for tonight,* Arthur thinks and unfolds his newspaper, scanning the headline that dominates the front page. The country has a new leader and the media talk of a real change coming to the world.

Anna comes over to him and reads from over his shoulder.

"Isn't it exciting, darling?" she coos and kisses him again on the cheek. This only increases Arthur's discomfort. He has begun chewing on a second mouthful of bacon and cannot properly reply. The mumbling he produces as a response, reminds him briefly of the shape of his mouth in the dream and a small, silent terror explodes like a tiny light bulb in his brain.

"I have to be off to the hairdressers," explains Anna. "Jennifer has gone shopping with her friends, so you'll have a bit of peace and quiet this morning."

Arthur watches as Anna pulls on her jacket and grabs the spare set of keys from the table.

"Have a good day, birthday boy. Don't be late home tonight!" she winks at him.

Arthur swallows the bacon and makes another sound in his throat.

"But, I'm not going anywhere," he protests.

His wife pulls a face. "What nonsense! I think you'll want to go for a drive, won't you?" She nods at the car keys that lie by a vase of flowers.

Arthur squints at the unfamiliar shape of the keys as his wife clicks out into the hall and he hears the front door close behind her.

On the stereo, Nina Simone strikes up again.

"Everything must change. Nothing stays the same. Everything must change. No-one, no-one stays the same."

Arthur frowns. The remnants of the poached egg glare up at him like a single yellow eye.

✳

"Morning, Neighbour."

Arthur does not answer Ned's greeting as he stumbles outside, still cloaked in his dressing gown, a slice of buttered toast in one hand and the unfamiliar keys in the other.

The toast falls to the ground, butter side up, as Arthur's eyes widen.

The car in the drive is not his own.

It is a Camaro, the kind he has admired for many years but which always seemed impractical for a family. He looks down at the keys and half understands.

How has she done this? How can they afford it?

For now, at least, he decides that these questions can wait.

He presses the automatic tracking button on the keys and hears a satisfying click and double beep as the Camaro responds.

He smiles broadly and turns back to the front door, intending to go inside and get dressed before taking the car out for a spin.

As he does so, he catches the eyes of Ned, who stands by the lawnmower, staring blankly back at him.

"Morning, Ned," says Arthur.

Ned does not reply, instead he continues to stare silently at Arthur.

Ned switches on the lawnmower and Arthur steps inside and closes the door behind him, suddenly very much aware of the cold.

✳

Arthur Kovic wipes the sweat from his forehead and tries to remain calm. He has been driving for several hours now and knows that he is completely and utterly lost. A deep fog has rolled in across the endlessly unravelling highway and he strains his eyes to pick out the roadside signs that flash by him. Confused

69

and afraid he switches on the radio, seeking guidance about this abrupt and unusual turn in the weather.

Instead of a weather report, a famous rock and roll singer from the 1970's is singing a song about changes and Arthur focuses on the familiarity of the voice, letting it soothe and reassure him, as cars flash by in streams of soft neon light.

He thinks about Anna, sitting at home, glaring at the clock, as she assures the party guests that the birthday boy will be home at any minute. How long, he wonders, will it be before she has to start making excuses for his absence and what ramifications will those excuses have on him when he eventually arrives home… *if* he arrives home?

A light begins to flash on the Camaro's dashboard indicating that he is running out of gas and Arthur makes a tiny, muted sound in the back of his throat. He turns up the headlights to full beam to combat the fog and sighs with relief when he sees a sign flash by advertising a gas station, a little under a mile up ahead. He looks at the meter ticking towards empty and reassures himself that it should be enough. Forcing himself to take deep breaths, he switches off the radio, just as the song ends and an advertisement for a new form of dental hygiene takes its place.

✹

"You've taken a wrong turning," explains the gas station attendant as he pumps the diesel into the car.

One by one, the attendant outlines Arthur's mistakes to him and carefully traces out the route he will have to take if he is to find his way back home.

Arthur watches the attendant replace the pump and hands the man his credit card. The attendant looks at him as if he has just handed him a particularly difficult quadratic equation.

"What's this for?"

"The gas."

Arthur watches as the attendant's previously cheerful face dissolves into a scowl.

"Okay, buddy. Where's the hidden camera?"

"I'm sorry?"

"You will be sorry if you don't pucker up and pay."

Arthur has never heard 'pucker up' used like this before and thinks the gas station attendant must be misusing it. A more pressing concern, however, is the problem with the card. Arthur feels the sweat rising on his brow as the attendant continues to glare at him. *The station must only take cash*, he reasons, *but, if that's the case then why is the attendant being so aggressive?* He fumbles for his wallet, digs around inside and is relieved to see that he has just enough in loose bills to cover the price of the gas.

The attendant hands him back the credit card, shakes his head in apparent distaste and returns to his duties.

Arthur stands alone in the moonlight, looking down at the credit card in his hands. There is nothing printed on the surface. It is as smooth and blank as an eggshell. He turns it over. There is no signature. No microchip.

Arthur puts it back into his wallet, gets back into the car and starts the engine. He grips the wheel tightly to stop himself from trembling.

✳

Arthur sees the lights flicker on in the living room window, as he carefully reverses up the gravel drive and brings the Camaro to a halt.

Ned stands by the lawnmower, exactly where Arthur left him this morning. He has a can of Coca Cola in his hand and Arthur notes with mild disinterest that Ned has apparently shaved off his trademark beard.

"Evening, Neighbour," says Ned.

Arthur does not answer.

The front door is already opening.

Anna beats on him with the flats of her hands as he tries to enter. Her mascara stained cheeks stand out against the shock of blonde hair that now rests where, only this morning, her dark brown locks hung. He does not like what she has done to herself, but he knows that this is not the time to say so. She listens to his rambling apologies but they seem as incomprehensible to him as to anyone else. He has driven the same route every day for the past five years and cannot explain how he came to lose his way today; how the roads seemed different and the signs to places he used to consider familiar led only to a strange, fog-infested highway with no end.

Anna screams and yells at him. She has been drinking and her words slur together. He tries to show her the blank, formless credit card, as if it will somehow explain everything, but she bats it from his hands and pushes past him up the staircase. From the top of the hall he hears their bedroom door slam shut.

Alone now, he looks around at the empty living room, noticing, for the first time, the banners that hang limply from the ceiling and the door to the kitchen. He notes the cake that sits, uneaten on the kitchen table and the empty glasses that embarrassed guests to a party that never happened have left behind them.

Arthur sits for a long time at the kitchen table turning the blank credit card over and over in his hands.

Eventually, he grows tired and creeps quietly up the staircase to brush his teeth. Before he heads to bed he opens the door to Jennifer's room, the passageway light illuminates it just enough to avoid waking her. He wanders softly over to her bedside and looks down at her sleeping, unmoving form.

The girl in the bed is not his daughter.

It is the other girl: The girl from the dining room who smelled of freshly cut grass, who wore her hair in dark brown pigtails and poked her tongue out at him from above the drawing of a butterfly.

Arthur hears the girl's voice in his head.

"Why are you afraid of butterflies?"

He stands unblinking in the half light, trembling over the girl's quietly sleeping form. From next door he can already hear Anna snoring loudly.

Someday

Arthur Kovic wakes and makes love to a blonde haired woman that is not his wife.

The bedroom is the same. The wallpaper is the same design that they picked out eight years ago. The bed is the same one that they purchased and spent a day assembling, just a few summers back, but the woman now straddling him is not his wife and not the mother of his daughter, Jennifer.

After it is over, he lies in the ruins of his marital bed, mired in the disgrace of the deed. Arthur is ashamed of what he has done: Ashamed of the suppressed lust that Anna's migraines have built up within him. He lies imprisoned and immobilised by his guilt. Eventually, he hears the radio turn on in the kitchen downstairs and Nina Simone's voice once again rising up to greet him.

"Everything must change. Nothing stays the same. Everything must change. No-one, no-one stays the same."

Now he can smell bacon frying on the pan. Now he can hear the crackle of the fat as it bursts and pops. Now he can hear the sounds of the woman, this stranger, this interloper, moving around downstairs and humming to herself.

He hauls his legs over the side of the mattress, and, pulling on his dressing gown, creeps downstairs.

A plate of bacon and eggs sits waiting for him at the kitchen table and the blonde woman, wearing one of Anna's dresses, smiles at him as he approaches.

"Morning, darling," she says.

It is Anna's voice.

Arthur Kovic sits down at the table and stares at the woman as she bustles about, laying out a second and third plate of bacon and eggs.

Arthur looks down at the plate. The woman has assembled the bacon and the eggs to look like a face. The face appears to be frowning.

Arthur tentatively begins his breakfast. The bacon looks and tastes peculiar and the eggs are bitter and far too large. He wonders what animal laid them. He opens his mouth to say something, then pauses as the dark-haired girl, wearing his daughter's nightdress, enters the kitchen, yawns and sits down at the table opposite him.

"Morning, Father," she says, without looking at him and takes a long slurp from a glass of orange juice.

Arthur looks at the strange, brown haired girl for a long time.

"Good Morning… Jennifer," he mutters, at last.

He tries hard to make the greeting sound like something other than a question.

✻

"Morphing, neighbours."

Ned's greeting has become as familiar as to almost go unnoticed, and so Arthur tells himself that he merely misheard and returns it, without looking at the man standing in the garden.

His 'wife' drives them to church. This happens after Arthur finds himself unable to start the car, unable to remember which of the wheels to turn and which of the buttons to press. His wife tells him not to worry; suggests that he is merely stressed from the events of the night before. The car, she reminds him, is old and she suggests that they buy a new one. Arthur Kovic nods as they drive, only half listening. He is too absorbed in the unusual colour of the morning sky.

The preacher's sermon is long and confusing and Arthur struggles to take it in; something about yeast and leavened bread. Arthur wishes that he was back in his greenhouse tending to his tomato plants.

He flicks through the hymn book but finds it to be full of mistakes. He glances up at the board by the altar; at the hymns that will be sung during today's service.

4 'Onwards Christian Solstice.'
8 'Colours of Moon'
16 'Amazing Grapefruit'
42 'The Lord's my Gargoyle'

Arthur snaps the hymn book shut and closes his eyes. The preacher reminds the congregation in his dulcet, dreary murmur, that God answers all prayers, but that sometimes the answer is 'no'.

When the Mass is over, Arthur and his 'family' drive to a small fast food outlet. Arthur is hungry but he cannot bring himself to eat. His 'wife' and 'daughter' eat the burgers and fries between them. It is dusk when they return home and the pigeons are cooing to one another from the treetops.

"Evening all," says a voice from across the hedge.

Arthur does not reply; does not look at the thing that stands, shuffling, by the lawnmower. Instead he heads inside and, without removing his shoes, marches straight through the house and out of the back door, into the serenity of the back garden and the security of the greenhouse.

It is calm in here and warm. Quietly, Arthur feeds his tomato plants, stumbling, as he does so, on the chrysalis that he first noticed on the previous evening. Delicately, he holds it up to the light, examining the small, translucent creature growing and changing, shifting and struggling within.

"I *am* afraid of butterflies." says Arthur.

He stands for perhaps minutes, perhaps hours this way, absorbed in this thought. Finally he understands what he must do and, leaving the greenhouse, he wanders over to the rain barrel in the corner of the garden, plunges his hand down into the cold, stagnant water and silently drowns the chrysalis.

Oneday

Arthur sits at his desk and examines his grey trembling hands. Nothing has come of his murderous act. He works long hours now and doesn't enjoy going home anymore.

The picture of his family that once proudly adorned his desk now lies hidden away in a desk drawer. After what he saw last time, Arthur does not care to look at it again.

Throughout the day a succession of people wander in and out of his office to deliver various bits of paperwork to him. They speak a language that he has long ago given up trying to understand. Sometimes the odd word is recognisable but it is nothing that gives him hope.

He continues to stare at his hands, trying to remember on which day it was that he woke up with the extra fingers. He can't remember. Even the names of the days have deserted him.

Arthur continues staring at his hands, as the door opens and he hears the familiar garbled voice of his boss. The words make no sense, but Arthur doesn't care. He knows what the message is; indeed he has been waiting for it for some time.

He is to be fired from his job of fifteen years for gross negligence. For weeks now, he has been burning the paperwork, tearing it up, letting it flutter from his office window or defacing it with obscene words. It has been his way of fighting back; of challenging the world to pay attention; demanding it notice him.

Arthur continues to stare at his grey, bulbous hands as the madman in the room bellows his indecipherable furies.

Finally, after a seemingly insurmountable period of time, Arthur looks up.

Finally, he screams.

Today

The kitchen is cool this evening. Arthur reasons that this is probably for the best, as the doctors say that he should stay out of the sun. On the television, a nature documentary shows the mating rituals of an unusual breed of animals. His daughter giggles and is scolded by his wife. She turns to him, her proboscis dripping mucus back into her bowl.

"Gorbol spake brackenhjev?" she asks, tilting her bulbous brow.

Arthur pauses, pushing his 'food' about awkwardly.

"Te...Teto, bre... bracken hobblescop," he tentatively replies.

His wife nods and resumes slurping at her gruel. The words mean nothing, of course. He makes them up as he goes along. It is better than to embarrass himself with silence.

He turns to his daughter, who, in a wry act of rebellion, pokes out what might be a tongue at him, and he is reminded, ever so briefly of a dream he had, many years ago.

It was a peculiar dream; lucid and so real, about a strange looking creature from another world called Arthur Kovic and the everyday mundane life this man led with his family, in a small, rural suburb where life was easy and nothing...*nothing* ever changed.

Maybe, tonight I will dream the dream again, he thinks.

The thought warms him and, done with his 'food', he rises from the table and wanders outside to inspect his tomatoes.

Michael Teasdale is an English writer from Newcastle upon Tyne. He has enjoyed spells living in Sweden, Vietnam and China and currently lives on the island of Ko Samui with a nice American lady and their two cats. He has previously written for *Novel* Magazine and *Litro* Magazine in the UK.

Targets

Eric Brown

Art: Jessica Good

I was watching the three-dee with Kelly when the programme was interrupted.

"Uh-oh," she said.

I gripped her hand. "Don't worry."

She turned and stared at me, the hologram pulsing on her forehead.

I stared at the three-dee in the corner. The frame was empty; then a tall man in a black suit appeared.

Kelly began to weep.

The suit said, "Citizens, your son, Edward, has been selected by LAPD for immediate targeting. Please make an appointment at your closest LAPD clinic within the next five days. I will now return you to *Sunny Days in Idaho...*"

Kelly jumped up and crossed to the bedroom door. I joined her, staring in at our sleeping son. He was curled up, warm and dreaming. Innocent.

"Was I a fool, Joe, for thinking...?"

I scratched my forehead where the hologram was. "We *both* hoped, Kelly. We dreamed."

I wondered at the chances of the child of two targets being selected. A statistical anomaly, I told myself.

We killed the three-dee and went to bed.

I couldn't sleep. At two, with Kelly sound asleep beside me, I rolled out of bed, dressed quietly and left the apartment.

It was a risk. Venturing out after dark was always a gamble for people like me and Kelly – and for Edward, now. But I needed a drink; more, I needed to talk.

I kept to the shadows, skulking like a rat. I knew where the night cops usually patrolled, but you could never be sure. Sometimes they liked to ring the changes, to keep people like me on their toes.

The bar wasn't signed. It was underground, literally. I crept down the steps, entered the code on the door and slipped inside.

It was like coming home.

A dozen people like Kelly and me, holograms glowing in the semi-darkness, sat quietly drinking.

I ordered a beer and drank. Thirty minutes later, I ordered another. I felt a little better then. At three, Al came in, fresh off his night shift.

"Hey, my friend." He clapped me on the shoulder. "Whatcha doin' here?"

I told him about Ed's selection.

He pulled a face. "Hey, that's tough. I'm sorry. How's Kelly?"

I shrugged. "Cut up. What do you expect?"

"That's life, Joe. We gotta learn ta live with it."

"Yeah," I said, and bought a couple of drinks. "Shit."

A few beers later, I staggered home. I kept to the shadows, but I wasn't afraid now. Dutch courage. Let the cops shoot me. Only tomorrow, when I'd sobered up, would I regret my foolishness, regret potentially making Kelly a widow at twenty-three.

So we took Ed to the LAPD clinic, and a blank-faced nurse zapped our son with the laser and a neat, round hologram target implanted itself in the centre of his forehead.

Our life changed, after that. No more risks. With Ed's welfare to think of, we imposed a curfew on ourselves. Never go out after sunset, only during the day; keep to busy areas. Avoid patrol cars, and don't *ever* go anywhere near police stations.

We got by.

Ed was bullied at school, of course. I remember the time I'd been singled out for the hologram on my forehead, and I felt powerless to help him. Words were useless. He had to learn to look after himself, just as Kelly and I, and all the others had done.

He grew into a great kid.

One day – he was around seven, eight – he came in after school and said, "Dad, I want to be a teacher when I grow up."

I could have wept. "That's great, Ed."

I glanced into the kitchen to see if Kelly had heard. She was facing the sink, her back tensed.

He'll forget the ambition in time, I told myself, move on to something else.

That night, in bed, Kelly said, "You gonna tell him he can't be a teacher?"

Years passed. We survived. I got a little heavier. My job at the landfill was steady. Kelly moved from Walmart to Safeway.

We began to think about what Ed might do when he left school at fifteen. I had a word with my boss, trying to get him a place at the landfill. Kelly's boss said there might be an opening stacking shelves in a few years.

One night, I was late back from the landfill. Just twenty minutes, but it nearly cost me my life. I was turning the corner to my block when I heard an engine behind me. The car was crawling along. My belly flipped.

I didn't turn, just walked faster.

The car drew alongside. A cop car.

Oh, Christ...

The driver said, "Stop right there and turn around real slow."

I did that.

The fat cop grinned. "Hey, look what we got ourselves here, Gene. If it ain't a fuckin' target."

His partner leaned forward, took a long look at me.

The driver said, "ID."

I passed him my card.

He scanned it, passed it back. I could see him calculating. Shoot me now, through the head, or have a little fun, let me run and get me in the back...?

"You work at Macready's landfill?"

"That's right, sir."

He said to his buddy, "We ain't stiffed no one from the 'fill in years, have we?"

"Don't think we have at that," Gene said.

He passed me my ID. "Off you go, boy."

I turned, shaking, and began walking. I thought of Kelly, making dinner at home. I thought of Ed, and the girl he'd been seeing lately...

I tensed myself for the bullet. *Just make it quick,* I thought. *In the head...*

The cop car started up. Caught up with me and drove alongside. The driver laughed. "Your lucky day, boy! You thank your fuckin' god I ain't in the mood."

They drove off, laughing, and it was all I could do to stop myself yelling obscenities after the bastards.

Ed was thirteen when he came home one day and said, "Dad, it's unfair."

I shrugged. "Life is unfair, Ed."

"But *why...?*"

"The country's overpopulated, Ed. The cops need to meet their quota."

"I suppose I meant... why me? Why us?"

I didn't like the whine in his voice. I shrugged again. "Why not? Life's a lottery. You take the good with the bad. It's no good complaining."

"But..."

"There's nothing you can do," I said. "End of. Learn to live with it. Do you hear your mom complain? Me?"

"I just wish..."

I sighed. "Try not to wish, Ed," I said. "Just accept."

Life wasn't that bad. We had the apartment. It was warm in winter, cool in summer. I had the job, my friends down the bar. Every month, I took Ed to a game. I felt safe in the crowd. I had Kelly, a woman who loved me, and a son who was growing into big, kind, bright young man.

I watched the news, but didn't take much notice. There was nothing I could do to make anything better. The way I looked at it, the world had always been going to hell in a handcart – so why worry? Just accept.

Ed left school and got a job at Safeway. He walked in every morning with Kelly, and came back with her at six. The extra income bought us a few luxuries: takeaways at the Thai place that had just opened along the block, and a subscription to one of the big cable channels

I was fifty, and I'd never been happier in my life.

One day, Kelly and Ed were late back from work.

I tried not to worry, but they were *never* late.

I called Kelly's cell phone. No reply. The same with Ed's.

Six-thirty came and went, then seven. I tried calling them again.

I turned on the three-dee, tried to watch a documentary about the Arctic.

Jesus... Eight o'clock.

They'll be fine, I told myself. Kelly's just got herself some overtime, that's all, and Ed's helping her, and they're so damned busy they haven't had time to call.

Then the image of the Arctic faded.

I stared at the guy in the black suit, my heart racing.

He stared back at me. I told myself he was just a virtual construct, not a real person with feelings. But that didn't stop me hating the bastard.

"I regret to inform you..."

I interrupted.

"Who?" I said. "Kelly, or Ed?"

Eric Brown has won the British Science Fiction Award twice for his short stories, and his novel *Helix Wars* was shortlisted for the 2012 Philip K. Dick award. His latest novel is *Murder Take Three*. He writes a regular science fiction review column for the *Guardian* newspaper and lives in Cockburnspath, Scotland. His website can be found at: www.ericbrown.co.uk

SF Caledonia: Chris Kelso

Our SF Caledonia editor Monica Burns is taking a break to allow her to concentrate on her Masters at the University of Dundee. This gives me a chance to introduce you to an up-and-coming Scottish writer, Chris Kelso.

Chris is a writer, a poet, an editor, a musician. He sold his first story at the age of 23 – he is now 29 – to the *Evergreen Review*. His works skitter around the edges of the definition of science fiction, often tending towards the weird and with a definite nod to the New Wave science fiction of the 60s and 70s. He does horror too. He is always experimenting with form, structure and flow, but always with characters you'd like to meet – or rather not, in lots of instances.

Chris is a busy man: he has five novels: *The Black Dog Eats the City*, *The Dissolving Zinc Theatre*, *Unger House Radicals* and the upcoming *Shrapnel Apartments* and *I Dream of Mirrors*.He has eight novellas: *A Message from the Slave State*, *Moosejaw Frontier*, *Transmatic*, *Last Exit to Interzone*, *Rattled by the Rush*, *Wire & Spittle*, *The Folger Variation*, and *The Church of Latter Day Eugenics* (jointly written with Tom Bradley). There are two short story collections: *Schadenfreude* and *Terence, Mephisto and Viscera Eyes*. Chris has also edited a few anthologies: *Terror Scribes*, *Caledonia Dreaming* (edited with Hal Duncan, *Slave Stories* and *This is NOT an Anthology,* which featured previously unpublished work by William Burroughs, Gerard Malanga and art by Clay S Wilson.

The Black Dog Eats the City was listed in Weird Fiction Review's best of 2014 and *Unger House Radicals* won the Ginger Nuts of Horror Novel of the Year award 2016

Most of Chris' work is published by American and Canadian publishers, something which *Shoreline of Infinity* is sorting: we have published the digital edition of *The Folger Variation and Other Lies*, and we will be publishing *I Dream of Mirrors* at some point in the near future. Most of Chris' works are available through Amazon.

I met Chris at a Speculative Bookshop event in Glasgow last year, where he placed a copy of *The Folger Variation and Other Lies* into my hands. When I finally reached that point in my to-read pile, I was immediately sucked in and held captive by the freshness of his writing and the apparent ease with which he draws his characters and settings. Chris gives them a twist of reality which brings them screaming into life and imprints them firmly into your brain. I swear I know Pancake Patterson from the Folger Variation.

I have since met Chris a few times, and got to know him a little. He's calmly energetic, quietly modest, and a pleasure to talk to. He looks so young – far younger than his often worldly-wise stories would lend you to believe. If I ever go to his house, I will not venture to look for paintings in his attic.

As a way for you to meet him, we exchanged emails, and here is a result of that. We've included an abridged extract from *The Folger Variation and Other Lies*.

-Noel Chidwick

Noel Chidwick: How would you describe your early years growing up, and do your experiences influence you as a writer?

Chris Kelso: I was a bit of a depressed kid – well, yeah, that would be an understatement. I got bullied quite a bit. I had milk-bottle specs and a crazy blonde bowl haircut. I was socially inept, majorly introspective and terrified of absolutely e-v-e-r-y-thing. Leaving my home town of Cumnock for Kilmarnock was enormously stressful. I had to join a new school, and I had to grow up fast. Predictably, the bullying intensified and I retreated into literature, arty films, weird music and, of all things, an obsession with football (which still didn't make me any more popular I should add!). It's strange, I still feel like that young boy on the receiving end. I'm much better at hiding my insecurities now though. Christ, I think I'd have bullied myself if I went back in time! I was this ridiculous, spectral presence. I brought most of the misery on myself, not that it excuses the victimisation – but it got to the stage where I enjoyed being left out. It gave me an excuse to explore the darkness further.

NC: Can you tell us a bit about your writing and motivations?

CK: In my books I am always writing from the perspective of the outsider. Of someone looking in from the outside. Someone trying to squint through the darkness for the tiniest mote of light. The underdog fascinates me – I am Scottish I suppose! It's much more interesting for me to drag tortured psyches through bizarre alien landscapes. Maybe I'm trying to make my own superhero, one who succeeds without donning a spandex suit or obtaining superhuman abilities. I actually find Peter Parker much more interesting when he's just a put-upon snot-nosed kid. If he'd managed to outwit the Green Goblin or Dr Octopus without the radioactive spider bite he would've been much more relatable. I'm not so much interested in the protagonist overcoming adversity, although I realise that's a depressing read for most people. I'm interested in how failure changes people. How they deal with abject rejection and heartache.

NC: When did you start writing? What kind of stories did did you write at the beginning?

CK: I was probably 8 or 9. I wrote a crazy story about this alien, made of bogies, who came to earth and took up residence in the mucus-filled caves of a human boy's nose. My primary 4 teacher was really disturbed by it and I seem to remember her using it against me at a parents evening chat with my parents – but I wrote the story straight faced! I wasn't trying to upset anyone or come off glib, I just wanted to write about an alien made of bogeys. To me it was legitimate short story subject matter.

NC: It's always fascinating to find out which books and authors kickstarted a writer's imagination - what books were you reading as a teenager? Which writers inspired you into becoming a writer?

CK: I was reading anything transgressive or dark – I was a pretty depressed young man, Noel. When I sit down and think about it, I graduated from the Goosebumps books, to 2000AD comics, to fairly extreme adult literature in a relatively short space of time. I distinctly remember thinking *Lanark* by Alasdair Gray was the ultimate pinnacle of artistic achievement at 16 – I still kind of think that to be honest. I remember *Naked Lunch* by Burroughs and a lot of Samuel Delaney's work (his non-SF stuff, like *The Mad Man* and *Hogg*) all having a profound influence, they were eye opening, unapologetic. At 17 there was *Blood and Guts in High School* by Kathy Acker and a LOT of Bukowski – this was my 'punk' phase. From there I ran the course of the new wave, speculative writers with something interesting to say and saying it in an interesting, confrontational way really appealed. *Dangerous Visions* [edited by Harlan Ellison] was a game changer. It introduced me to Philip José Farmer and Michael Moorcock and I measure my prose up to their standard every time. I like that SF didn't have to be space operas and laser beams (although I have a soft spot for their naiveté as I approach 30). Introduce a brief love affair with the Russians and Hubert Selby Jr, and you've about got my teenage, post-university pallet to the letter. I had a healthy hodgepodge of inspirations.

But really, I've always wanted to be a writer, socialise with writerly people. I've always admired authors and fantasized about being one when I grew up, as young as 9 or 10 I remember that feeling. You basically get to sit around all day expressing your own little stories and occasionally selling them on to publishers. You get to pick a cool front cover and have someone else typeset the thing for you so it looks good. The life of a published author is pretty sweet, even if the money is awful! When it comes to ego fondling, there's not much that can top it. I think I've just always been into the lifestyle and the freedom of writing too. I really love sharing ideas and I think we achieve a whole different level of intimacy through creative collaboration. That's my idea of inspirational. Hope that doesn't sound trite.

NC: I'd describe your writing style as punchy, vibrant and direct. A distinctive writer's voice is important – how did your voice evolve and develop? Was it instinctive, or something you have worked on over time?

CK: It came out naturally. I

had a lot of pent-up frustration that I wasn't articulating. I'd just dropped out of university and my girlfriend had dumped me. I wrote like an angry little man with no filter. Writing was a release. It was therapeutic. I come across as much more self-assured in my narrative voices than in real life. Writing let me be other people, angry ones who wanted to revel in the abyss. It's not an affectation though. That self-assured, ballsy wee man is in me somewhere. He must be. Buried deep down maybe, shackled – but he's in there nonetheless. He comes out when I'm in front of a keyboard. Bloody lucky too.

I think I'd like to tame him a bit. He can be a bit of a force of nature and that's always exhausting for a reader. I think we're always trying to perfect a style and as an artist it's difficult not to pick holes in your own work. I would eventually like to write something that appeals to a wider audience. By that I don't mean write schmaltzy romance books or high fantasy, nor would I consider censoring myself – but I think the essence of what I'm trying to say isn't such an inaccessible idea (the idea that we want to belong to something, that we're pissing against the wind). I just need to crack the template that makes this concept appealing to a broader audience.

NC: You're obviously inspired by William Burroughs - what attracts you to that style of writing?

CK: Burroughs did whatever he wanted. He was a punk rock pioneer. At a time when I needed a real shot to the arm, a new hit, *Naked Lunch* came into my life. He experimented with narrative, with form and typeset. He made books into art objects. Plus, he just never seemed to give a shit. The writing was in your face and possessed a kind of punk energy. Basically it's everything I wish I was in real life but will never be. He can teach you a lot about being an artist and about integrity.

Burroughs was a superstitious fellow too; I relate to that. While I'm not religious at all, I do have some irrational beliefs. One tradition I've adopted from him is this – I finish the book, get it published then I never read that book again. If I *never* read the book again then it won't be a complete failure. I'm not even that superstitious. Depending on what your idea of failure is, I think it's a solid tradition that's seen solid results.

NC: Anything you wouldn't write about?

CK: Absolutely not. There is no subject I'll shy away from. I might alter the way I approach something just to make sure the writing doesn't come across as glib or totally insensitive, but generally – no – I won't back away from anything. I think I've covered most, if not all the taboo subjects, in my writing. Those are the subjects that are interesting!

In fact, I might steer clear of bestiality because, well, I just don't have the imagination to explore that particular area.

NC: So far your works are shorter novella/novelette length – when will we see the Chris Kelso pan-galactic space operatic six-volume box set?

CK: Ach, I'm not much of a Peter Hamilton-style writer. I keep my books mercifully brief. In saying that, I have just written a 300 pager – a sequel to my existential horror novel *Unger House Radicals*. It's the most ambitious project I've undertaken, and, astonishingly, it only took 4 months to write. Then there's *I Dream of Mirrors*. It's probably the most complete novel I've written, the most cohesive. It says everything I've been trying to say for years. I suppose it's taken me 12 books to get to this point and I've finally worked out how to communicate what I want to say.

NC: You write, you draw, you're a musician: do you envisage combining these talents into one project? If so, what would it be?

CK: Yes! There will be a project coming soon. I can't say much about it yet, but I've got the go-ahead to make my first comic book. The script is already finished. I've always been in and out of bands. I'm nowhere near good enough to be in a jazz band yet. When I become technically proficient enough I'll pack it all in and tour with a jazz troupe.

I have too many other interests though, it's debilitating. I'm a big cinephile too. I'd love to get a script produced. I came so close this one time and got burned. Then there's the insane stepson to consider. He's a bloody riot a minute.

NC: What are you working on at the moment, and what's about to appear?

CK: Loads of stuff! I have a ak of esoteric horror stories out with John Langan and Don Webb; a bizarro collaboration with Tom Bradley about a journalist who stumbles across London's sex-cult underbelly; *I Dream of Mirrors*, an existential SF novel, is with the esteemed editor Andrew J. Wilson and will be out through *Shoreline of Infinity* soon; I'm also editing a Seb Doubinsky tribute anthology. There's the sequel to *Unger House Radicals* called *Shrapnel Apartments* in amongst all that. Plus a bunch of other stuff in the pipeline. I just started an imprint of Rooster Republic called RoosterVision. It'll be similar to the Centipede Press non-fiction books about cinema and we'll be releasing the first book in about a month. It'll be a busy year.

NC: I'm looking forward to all this. Chris, thanks for your time.

The Folger Variation

abridged extract

Chris Kelso

Art: Chris Kelso

They say it was a gas leak that demolished both five-storey apartment buildings. The explosion blew out windows over a block away, sprinkled debris onto an elevated commuter railroad track and cast a mushroom cloud of smoke over the skyline. It was insane, took me almost four years to get over Deborah's death.

I hit the drink harder and harder, doing Dexedrine just to stay awake, throwing more anthracite onto the fire until I was sliding blindly through life on rivulets of my own bad judgement. When you lose love, at first anyway, it feels like the end of everything. Those four years remain a complete blur. I remember I found some incredible drugs during that period of roaming the wilderness. For a brief time I hung around with a gang of kids who loved Pancake Patterson and were obsessed with synthesising fictitious drugs – Korova milk bars (made with mescaline and opiates) and ephemerol (which were really just mushrooms ground into a paste). We'd take hits from asthma inhalers and store the drugs in ear drop containers. There was even this drug called SOAP that worked just like real soap, but when you bathed with it a microparticulate entered your pores and the high was, well, simply unparalleled – you had to be careful you didn't slump into your bath and drown though.

Those experiences were much less mind expanding than you'd think. People were off fighting in the Kinesis wars battling an alien virus of the mind, but I sometimes think the drugs we took did more harm to a man's brain than the poor soldiers on the battlefield who were getting crushed to smithereens, 10 synapses at a time. Miraculously I somehow managed to keep my position in the e-resource library. The library was the only real job I ever loved, I was grateful to've kept it. I know I bitched about it all the time but compared to other jobs I'd had it was a fuckin' cake walk! Course, before the library I'd worked as a ditch-digger for some Ursa Minor family funeral company, worked as a flunky on a freighter, built with huge girders and an expensive-looking armour plated deflector shield, that hung suspended in space like a hunk of deformed scrap metal – and as a dishwasher on one of those battlecruisers. I never saw any action from the wars, thank god! Every time it was the same deal. After a fortnight on the job I'd get that itch. I'd say – *Arty, why are you condemning your soul to suicide?* Then I'd pack the job in, toss my shovel or my keys or my apron in the direction of the boss and go – *see ya!* – casual as you like. Jesus, I was a ballsy little sonofabitch back then.

At the library I had a real sympathetic boss called Janine who did a great job covering my ass. I told her I was depressed but the truth was that by this stage I was blunt to the core. I will never forget Janine and all the strings she pulled.

Of course I contemplated using the time machine my grandfather gave me to go back in time to save Deborah, to prevent the Kinesis wars from ever happening, but I was terrified to use the damn thing. I didn't really think it worked yano, but I wasn't about to take the chance

✳

Eduardo was a porter working in a basement nearby, an older gent of about 55 with pockmarked skin and big dark eyes. He was originally from LA and claimed to've played Russian roulette with Pancake Patterson. Guess there was no reason to doubt him. I lived with him for a wee while. We originally met through snooker tournaments and started getting together at The Wifebeater every second Sunday when he had the night off.

Eduardo occasionally talked about the Kinesis Battles that swept through the US and detailed the coldness of war seeping into the mud and mortar of trenches in the machine gun night. He saw the brains of his comrades turned to fondue by enemy drones, saw their smoky, scooped-out eye sockets scoured of any recognisable humanity, tasted their burning flesh when the food ran out. Since the wars Eduardo had become a little slow. Apparently one of the viruses had caught him, put his brain in a vice-tight grip until fluid oozed from it like a wrung-out sponge. I don't know how he survived. He couldn't remember either. *What exactly did he fight for? What was he coming back for — a dead wife and a dead-beat son?*

I kept getting up every day for work. Sometimes I'd punch in late but at least I kept showing up. At the weekends I'd play snooker with Eduardo. He kept me on the straight. There's no way I could've pulled myself up from the mire without him. Gradually I got better. Started jogging and taking better care of myself. Deborah became a foggy memory that I was able to bury beneath folds of denial. I started appreciating the smellscapes around me, illuminating gases and banana oil. I still didn't bother with the time machine my cookie old grandfather gave me on his deathbed. I barely knew the guy, for all I knew he was off his rocker on medication. Scientists were doing amazing things, but time travel was never discussed. You never heard it mentioned man.

✳

When Eduardo died of a cardiac arrest I just sort of stuck around at his apartment. I found his body slumped over a chair in an odd position. I remember the sky had gone from grey to hot silver. Quarks of daylight broke through and cast an unflattering luminosity onto the southernmost features of his face. The roads outside were left like shallow rivers once the rain had ceased. I could've sworn I saw my hopes and dreams drift along the gutters. Even the neighbours seemed to think I'd always lived there. All evidence of Eduardo seemed to disappear from memory when he passed away. The police never checked in, neither did the rest of his family. An ambulance crew came by, took the body and that was that. There was no funeral.

I know, I know – you think I'm a parasite, right? Well, I was lonely and desperate as a fuckin' starving dog. I'd been doing so well to stay sober and motivated. People kept telling me to stay optimistic all the time. Optimistic? Optimistic? *I'm plenty optimistic* I'd tell them! But I remember thinking at the time – *how can anyone be optimistic? I'm a good man. I'm a GOOD man! I'm a good MAN! I told a few white lies in my life and that's all I can be blamed for! Why can't I catch a break, huh? Why do people I know keep dying?* I'd never felt so alone.

The Murderer

I explored the darkness farther, turned left down the hallway and saw the bassinet. A doughy faced kid rocked gently in slow-wave-sleep. I *had* to be quick. A violent and prolific murderer was on my tail. The murderer was someone I knew well – as well as the limp 4-month old I'd just scooped up to cradle in my arms.

I made for the open fire escape, tried my best not to alert anyone to my presence. I pulled in the familiar odour of front-load washing machine mould for what I hoped would be the last time. It was a miracle the baby hadn't woken up man, a goddamned miracle – my mother said I'd always been an eerily deep sleeper.

As I was resting my leading foot onto the steel gratings of the outside stairwell, my mother's scream rang out, compressing the air within the inner pillars of my ears until one of the drums P-P-POPPED! I thought about Deborah and the exploded apartment, the only other time I'd heard anything that loud before. In my panic, I accidentally jerked the baby awake and he was now wailing in unison with my mother. *Christ…* All the lights suddenly switched on and I was completely exposed. I stooped under the lower sash of the window and clamped loudly down each level on the platform. The rebound of a gunshot came from up in the apartment. My mother's screaming ceased. I knew the murderer was there and that my parents were both dead – *again*. The howling of stray dogs on the streets kept ice in my blood.

I reached the second floor, slid the final ladder down and descended to the street. The murderer kept eliminating every variation of Deborah, as if he was trying to take away the one thing that gave my life any meaning. Eventually I stopped trying to save her. All I could do man was try to save myself, you know? The baby continued to wail. I heard footsteps from above in close pursuit. I ran. I was used to running away, always escaping...

Walking Through the Fire

I met Jacob Falcon, a community fireman, antiquarian librarian and small press owner. He thought himself something of a dilettante. I remember he hated all the Ursa Minor chaps, hated the nail bars and hair salons they were opening on every corner at the expense of some vintage bookshop he'd held dear. He smelled of continental cigarettes and claimed to enjoy the taste of madeleines dipped in tea. The press was called 'Black Arrow' or 'Black Adder Books' or something like that. We met during a snooker game in *The Wifebeater*. I seemed to meet all the interesting cats in there. We got to talking (him mainly about his espousal of sweet Buddha) and before long he started pushing me to write a fuckin memoir—*might be therapeutic* he said. *Help you get over Debs* he said. Eventually I sat down with a second-hand tablet in Eduardo's back room and churned out a self-indulgent piece of clap-trap that Jacob reluctantly and begrudgingly sent to press and was later released as a limited edition eBook called *WALKING THROUGH THE FIRE*. The title was a reference to a Charles Bukowski collection and a quote that went – *what matters most is how well you walk through the fire*. At the time I thought it was pertinent as hell. Course, the majority of the book was a pack of lies; in fact the only interesting thing that had ever happened to me was the gory death of my wife Deborah. I'd let it define me. Hideous creatures continued to weave through the geometries of space and into my life.

Point being, I know it wasn't a masterpiece, but Jacob was putting out books by local herbalists and fortune tellers so I hardly think I lowered the quality of his fuckin' stock. He was a little too preoccupied with his upcoming trek out to El Paso to live across the river in a $49 a month cottage with his Buddha Bibles and legume dishes to really have any quality control. *WALKING THROUGH THE FIRE* didn't sell many if you can believe *that*, but it did win me the affection of a young kid called Leo. He was a wannabe writer and I guess he figured that cos I had a book out I was some kind of authority on the subject. *'Follow your inner moonlight, don't hide the madness'* – I told him, but what the fuck did I know? Exactly – nothin'! It was Ginsberg who said that!

Although I detested the book I never went back to erase it from history. Hell, I still wouldn't want it gone, even if I had the fuckin choice, yano?

Leo would always ask me if I had any tips for writing a memoir. I never really knew what to tell the kid but I sure enjoyed the attention and took him under my wing for a time. It felt good to have a protégée, it was different from being in love and being loved… it was more a one-way street that was going in my direction. I didn't have to give Leo a goddamn thing and he still held me in high-regard. I don't think anyone has ever thought that highly of me.

When he was in Eduardo's apartment one night I said to him that going through old keepsakes was a good way to provoke memories, get the creative juices flowing. Leo asked to see *my* memory box. That's when I came across my grandfather's trinket.

- What's that thing? – He asked, his dumb floppy fringe hanging over one side of his face. He must've noticed my reaction, the marble eyes bugging out, nostrils broadening, the complete whitewash of my complexion.

- What is it? – He asked again, a little louder this time with the intention of snapping me out of the trance.

- Something I've been running away from my whole life.

- How come?

- Truth is Leo my boy, if it works I'm not sure I entirely trust myself with its power…

Leo pushed me for more details but I said I was tired and he left.

✳

I kept having the same nightmare—the one where I came face to face with myself in a dark alleyway. Whenever I woke it was difficult to disassociate myself from the residue of my dream, the dark shapes streaking the wall with menacing intent. My mother called me. I got up, touched the keypad and the interface screen purled into life. I clipped the electrodes onto both my eyelids. There was a pop of static from the intercom and my mother's voice became clear.

- Your father is dead. Her voice had an inhuman quality that crackled, hissed and fluctuated like what electricity must sound like as it passes through wire.

I hung up.

A few days after discovering the device the e-resource library shut down because of poor business. I was destitute. Suddenly my grandfather's trinket seemed like an escape route...

Idle Hands

That night I took the trinket in my hand, fondled it for about half an hour. There was something about it, something dangerous, powerful. It seems ridiculous to say this, but it frightened me in a way I'd never experienced before. It was small and lightweight but had all the patterns of internal cogs and mechanisms visible through its metal frame. It had a tiny monitor that displayed nautical charts and terrestrial range radars, the detail was fuckin crazy. Course, if this really was a time travelling device then in some branching off of this reality all of *this* had already happened and I'd *already* made a decision. Right...?

My grandfather was a senile old coot who smelled of bread chemicals for some reason, a genius probably, but a boor and a heartless sonofabitch at the same time. My dad only ever knew him as this cold, withdrawn cat, always out in his shed trying to build things. I heard he made a robot boy once to replace my dad but it broke down and he never bothered going through all the hassle of rebuilding. For some reason granddad always seemed to like me, even if he didn't show it much, he seemed to have less animosity towards me than the rest of the family. I was secretly quite pleased when he died. I think my dad was too.

Turns out the trinket worked like a drug. There was a tiny nozzle inside about the size of a pinprick and it ejaculated a clear substance in close proximity to human flesh. I fed a polypropylene needle into the nozzle and descended the plunger. The fluid glittered in the syringe barrel like burning intergalactic pulsars. My stomach was in knots but I knew I had to get a hold of myself – *this is your one chance to get out of this place you crazy idiot* – I kept saying. So I mainlined a vein (got that old familiar feeling, ready for a bit of ultraviolence) and administered the time travelling fluid. It's quite a feeling, the evisceration of every particle in your body and its subsequent regeneration in a different region of time.

The Prophet of Tolerance

Hell's Kitchen in the 2070's was a profoundly dangerous place, especially at night, man. I knew at this rate I'd surely be spotted. Even at quarter past midnight, The Rite Aid pharmacy lights were still on, the food emporiums and arcades ever-glittering with activity. Extra-terrestrial kids played midnight baseball behind cages (or their own alien equivalent at least) and the streets and alleyways were jam-packed with nefarious Midtown West types trying to secure prostitutes or Jam-Caps. There was nowhere to hide in this part of town when you'd just kidnapped a baby.

I ducked into a narrow alley and tried to catch my breath. I clung to the screaming child with an almost maternal robustness. There was a young kid, maybe seventeen or eighteen years old, sprawled across a bed of garbage, but he was too out-of-it to pose any kind of threat. I rested the baby on my knee and tried to calm it down. A fire engine klaxon annoyed me as it hurtled past.

- Please! I'm begging you, man, just stop crying for a damn minute…

But the restless baby's wails did not falter, man, no siree. The polytonal urban chorus was relentless. The comatose bum jolted back to life, angry that he'd been awoken from his drug-induced slumber. He started gesticulating and babbling drunkenly.

- Hey, you gotta be quiet! Listen, you want some money? You want some, man?

I tried to forward the young bum some crushed notes but the kid was apoplectic. I had to shut him up somehow, considered burying a switchblade into his abdomen, just above his pelvis – after all, who would miss a lousy derelict like *this* guy? Something stopped me, the kid's face was starting to look familiar, even in the eclipsed alley; a certain oblate chubbiness to him that prickled the tiny hairs on the back of my neck.

I remembered, while visiting Elfreth's Alley in 1723, encountering a 17 year old, and impoverished, Ben Franklin newly arrived in Philadelphia from New York. I showed Franklin a hundred dollar bill with his face on it and promised that everything would work out ok for him. The ranting hobo in my wake looked eerily similar, to the point where I actually screwed up my eyes and was about to utter the name – *Ben?*

Suddenly the young bum stopped his inane blethering. A puncture of blood appeared directly between his eyes and trickled down the left hand side of his cheek. The bum's legs buckled and he fell forward, face first, into his bed of trash, his head smacking off of an egg-crate buried beneath. I turned to see a silhouetted figure in the alley.

- Arty... I got you now, you sonofabitch. There's nowhere to go.

The Beachcomber

Mark Toner

and

Stephen Pickering

HMM... LOOK WHAT HAS *WASHED UP* ON THE SHORELINE *TODAY* – A SOMEWHAT *OVERPOWERED* RAY GUN BELONGING TO ...

SPACE ENFORCER 3000

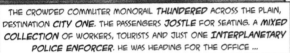

THE CROWDED COMMUTER MONORAIL *THUNDERED* ACROSS THE PLAIN, DESTINATION *CITY ONE*. THE PASSENGERS *JOSTLE* FOR SEATING. A *MIXED COLLECTION* OF WORKERS, TOURISTS AND JUST ONE *INTERPLANETARY POLICE ENFORCER*. HE WAS HEADING FOR THE OFFICE ...

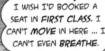

I WISH I'D BOOKED A SEAT IN *FIRST CLASS*. I CAN'T *MOVE* IN HERE ... I CAN'T EVEN *BREATHE*.

... AND THE *TRAIN* WAS *LATE!*

I *HATE* COMMUTING. IT'S SO *POINTLESS*. *HOURS* OF MY LIFE *WASTED* ON A CROWDED MONORAIL.

SIGH!

I WISH THESE *NUMBSKULLS* WOULD QUIT *PUSHING* ME. THEY HAVE *NO* RESPECT.

HEY! WATCH WHERE YOU'RE *POKING* THAT *UMBRELLA*, YOU *BIG DOPE!* YOU COULD HAVE SOMEBODY'S *EYE OUT!*

I KNOW *YOUR TYPE.* USING THE *PRETEXT* OF TRYING TO *PUSH* PAST ON *CROWDED TRAINS,* WHEN *ALL* YOU'RE TRYING TO *DO* IS *RUB YOURSELF* AGAINST *INNOCENT LITTLE OLD LADIES.*

BE OFF WITH YOU!

I'LL HAVE YOU KNOW I'M AN *INTERPLANETARY POLICE ENFORCER,* ON A MISSION TO *SAVE THE UNIVERSE* FROM *SUBVERSIVE ALIEN LIFE FORMS.*

YOU *DON'T FOOL* ME. YOU'RE JUST A *DIRTY OLD MAN* IN A *RUBBER SUIT* AND, IF YOU DON'T GO AWAY, I'LL *CALL* THE *GUARD* AND HAVE YOU *THROWN OFF!*

I'VE NEVER HEARD *ANYTHING* SO *RIDICULOUS* IN *MY LIFE! NOW,* MOVE OVER AND LET ME *SIT DOWN* ON *THAT SEAT.* I HAVE THE *AUTHORITY* YOU KNOW.

DON'T YOU TELL *ME* TO *MOVE OVER!* I'M *OLD ENOUGH* TO BE *YOUR MOTHER!* TAKE *ONE STEP CLOSER* AND I'LL *SCREAM* THE *ROOF* OFF THIS *CARRIAGE.*

IS THIS MAN *ANNOYING* YOU, MADAM?

I'VE BEEN *LISTENING* FROM *BACK HERE.*

YES! HE *SAYS* HE'S SOME SORT OF *POLICE OFFICER* BUT HE'S BEEN *TRYING* TO *RUB* HIMSELF *AGAINST* ME.

HE *DID,* DID HE? *WE'LL SEE* ABOUT *THAT!*

OOOF!

It's *TOUGH* being an *INTERPLANETARY POLICE ENFORCER*. They never told me *HOW TOUGH* when I was at *TRAINING COLLEGE*.

I THOUGHT IT WOULD BE ALL *GLAMOUR*, RESCUING DISTRESSED *MOON MAIDENS* FROM SLAVERING *BUG EYED MONSTERS*.

SAVING THE *PLANET* FROM *DEATH RAY BEAMS* IN THE *NICK OF TIME*.

I WAS HOPING FOR MORE *PUBLIC ADULATION*. EVEN A BIT OF *APPRECIATION* WOULDN'T GO AMISS.

INSTEAD I GET *THROWN OFF THE TRAIN* AND HAVE TO *WALK* TO WORK. *HEAVEN KNOWS* WHAT MY *BOSS* WILL SAY WHEN I *FINALLY* GET TO *WORK*.

WHERE THE HELL HAVE YOU BEEN *NUMBER 4?!* PULL *YOURSELF* TOGETHER *MAN!* WE HAVE A *UNIVERSE* TO *SAVE!*

Number 4 Reading List
"Planet Stories" Spring 1942 Cover
Painting - Alexander Leydenfrost

"Planet Stories" July 1952 Cover
Painting - Allen Anderson

"American Splendor" Comic Series -
Harvey Pekar and Robert Crumb
(www.crumbproducts.com)

Noise and Sparks: The Legend of the Kick-Arse Wise Women

Ruth EJ Booth

This is how I thought it went:

You live first. You learn. You travel, explore the world, find your niche. You get the job. You find the one. You settle down, get married, have kids. Discover a whole new way of looking at things. Then – once you've done all that, once the kids are gone, and you've this huge wodge of life experience in the bank – that's when you get to write.

And I was happy with that. Even as the rest of my childhood dream crumbled, and the urge to write became insistent, I held onto the idea that the fun of writing fiction was for retirement. You needed experience to draw on to write with authority. And besides, without a pension to support me, how could I afford the time to do it?

These sound like excuses, but this was what I genuinely believed. I'd seen all those celebrated women writers on TV – the Ursula Le Guins, the Maya Angelous – all older women. It made sense it took a lifetime's worth of experience to write something true and universal. I was prepared to wait, if that's what it took to be that cool.

But I'd made three mistakes. The first was confusing the mastery of older writers for the wisdom of age, not the product of years spent honing their craft. The second was giving in to my fears. And the third, arguably the most important, was this: you don't get to choose when you have something to say.

The first will be familiar to anyone who's tried writing fiction. It springs partly from a common misconception: writing is easy, because it's something we all learned in school. The lie becomes obvious the moment you put pen to paper: writing takes years to master. Discouraging as it seems, it's a liberating lesson. There are no age restrictions. You can start at any time. All it takes is a willingness to work hard.

"you don't get to choose when you have something to say."

And hard it is: frustrating, sometimes to the point of tears, to spend hours crafting the perfect sentence, only to receive rejection after rejection upon sending it out. Embittering, if you can't resist comparing the success of your peers to your own, instead of celebrating with them. But these are distractions. There's an intrinsic joy in the act of creation, in making something that lives in the mind and in the heart: the very root of a love of writing.

Hard work didn't deter me. It's strange to think of it now: in my late twenties, freelance music writing, I'd try creating the odd bit of fan fiction, even sketching original ideas, and find myself absorbed by the work. But I'd never have any intention of taking them further. That was for later. Nor was I comparing myself to others – I had no connection to the fiction scene – but, because of that, no way of challenging my beliefs either.

Feminist readers may consider my childhood image misogynistic, as only allowing women their liberty once their reproductive use has passed. What I was conscious of was needing to tick those boxes of traditional womanhood first. Really, I couldn't wait to become one of those silver-haired kick-arse women.

But as I wrote those first tentative stories, my respect for experience warped into a mask for my fear of ridicule: less concerned that I was unready to write, more that people would know this if I tried. Respect must be earned – but surely no one could argue with experience! That was why new bands got heckled, wasn't it? That was why young academics in my old department played games of one-upmanship with their visiting peers, right? I wouldn't have to worry about wasting my time if I waited. They couldn't criticize me then.

If social media teaches us anything, it's that neither acclaim nor ability stops scorn. You may be a best-selling author, movie options coming out of your ears, but even Joanne Harris and J. K. Rowling experience daily trolling. Paying your dues doesn't end that. But again, I'd yet to see any of this. So, I'd just write the occasional story for my guildmates, get creative with music journalism, or devise alternative lyrics on fan forums. Just a bit of fun, I'd think, little realizing I was writing already.

See, I hadn't twigged that inspiration wasn't waiting 'til I hit my 60s. There's a reason for that – inspiration is the mind at work. The artistic process isn't simply triggered by breaching some experience threshold. It's the way we interpret the world around us, and process what's happened, allowing us to move on. To build up life experience without ever digesting it is akin to spending our lives eating, carting around our swollen bellies, and taking one glorious dump at the end of it all. However literally you take that, that can't be healthy.

And it had already begun to trickle out. All these things I'd been making, yet I hadn't realised I was already writing. Still I held back.

In the end, what made me abandon my plan was the death of my Grandmother. One of the original kick-arse wise ones for me, our Grandmother-from-Hell passed away after a lengthy illness, mid-way through an Art History course. She was so enthusiastic about it. She'd always put off going to university.

Her death knocked me for six, not least because we kids had always expected her to live forever. It gave the lie to my idea of the endless time I'd have at the end of my life to do the things I loved. I realised I really couldn't wait to become a kick-arse woman. There was only here and now.

So, I began to write in earnest. And once I did, things began to change. I started to think more clearly. I felt more comfortable in myself. The barrier I'd always felt between myself and the musicians I interviewed melted away – and with that, the other lies I'd held onto.

I realised I didn't need to earn the right to write, except by hard work. And I could have fun doing that! As I gained confidence and started going to conventions, I found a welcoming community of creative people who understood how I felt, friends whose company I hope I'll treasure for the rest of my life. To this day, I still wonder why I felt I had to wait to be this happy. I suspect I'll be unpacking that for years to come.

I still intend to be a silver-haired kick-arse wise woman when I'm older. I just don't want to have to wait 'til then to be content with my life. It's a choice that involves a lot of graft; a lot of frustration too, at times. Yet, unlike my age, the sheer luck involved in becoming successful, or the reactions of other people, that's one thing I can control.

Ruth EJ Booth is a BSFA award-winning author and academic, studying on the MLitt in Fantasy at the University of Glasgow. Her work can be found at www. ruthbooth.com

---

Reviews

All the Galaxies
Philip Miller
Freight Books, 308 pages
Review: Henry Northmore

Fans already know that many of the strongest works in the genre use sci-fi as a prism to examine our own world. Taking existing concepts and extrapolating into the future, exaggerating for effect or repositioning them on strange new worlds. We live in volatile political times offering plenty of meat for writers to chew over. However Philip Miller can't have known how timely *All the Galaxies* would be when published. Set after a second failed Scottish Independence Referendum (which could be as soon as 2018 if the SNP get their wish), in the following years the country descended into violence, known as 'The Horrors', then split into antonymous city states.

John Fallon is a disillusioned journalist at a Glasgow newspaper looking on aghast as the city he loves and the print media industry he has devoted his life too crumbles around him. Fallon's past is a tangle of messy relationships, his teenage son has gone missing and there are strange reports of a man with stigmata prowling a derelict tower block. These 'real world' stories form the core of *All the Galaxies* but are tinged with fantasy and intercut with the cosmic adventures of a boy and his dog as they travel across the universe.

This is Miller's second novel after 2015's *The Blue Horse*. He's a wonderful wordsmith. Some of his descriptions are beautifully evocative, filling the senses with detail. There's an early paragraph that sums up Miller's skill, succinctly capturing Fallon's work environment: "The smells of the newsroom. Old paper and the coughings of dust mites. Cold coffee and perfume. Polystyrene

mesh with the more grounded central narrative. It's an interesting aside that adds a dash of colour and pure sci-fi but can interrupt the flow of the main story.

There are several mysteries to keep you involved and Miller's rich characters, especially Fallon, are captivating. Scottish readers will find the setting and subject matter particularly pertinent but *All the Galaxies* is a universal story of missed opportunities, mistakes and human relationships with added space whales and too much whisky. The focus drifts from time to time, however Miller's mix of politics, social commentary and sci-fi is always beautifully written and engaging.

trays of abandoned food. Lank settled farts. Unpressed three-day-old shirts and earwax. A grey cloud of desperate gloom. The clinical smell of the broken photocopier."

The Mercury might be a fictional paper but Miller is a journalist, and works as an arts correspondent at Glasgow's daily broadsheet *The Herald*. He understands this world from the inside out, making several pertinent points about the future of journalism, the rise of the internet and its effect on writers and consumers of news content.

The Glasgow sections are riveting, his cast authentic and fully fleshed out, even as they sometimes drift into the realm of the supernatural. The young boy's interstellar journey fills far fewer pages, it's intriguing but less gripping. The identity of the mysterious astral traveller is fairly obvious from early on and while it links directly, it doesn't quite

The Last Days of New Paris
China Miéville
Del Rey, 224 pages
Review: Eris Young

Set against a backdrop of crumbling streets and burned-out buildings, *The Last Days of New Paris* follows the parallel stories of Thibault, the last surviving member of a rebel army of artists, and Jack, arrogant acolyte of occultist Aleister Crowley. As hostilities inside New Paris reach a stalemate, dark rumours spread of a nazi weapon with the power to turn the tide of the war. In order to stop it, Thibault and his mysterious companion Sam must navigate the streets of a city marred by war and black magic, and haunted by unearthly manifestations of surrealist art – and worse.

China Miéville loves cities – London, San Francisco, and now Paris – and he's adept at creating characters of them, embedding weirdness into the very bricks and mortar of a place with scientific precision and organic grace.

The last book of his I read was *Kraken*, which had a magic system as esoteric and visceral as any I'd ever encountered, and fully immersed me from the first page. The key to making a work of fantasy effective is to obscure the ordinary and elucidate the fantastic; Miéville excels at talking about objects and events that defy natural laws, making them almost banal, as if he's not imagining but *describing* them as he sees them: this is what gives his work its power.

In *The Last Days of New Paris*, Miéville again picks apart and re-stitches the fabric of reality, rendering New Paris as a wellspring of the bizarre, as if the pavement and bricks are merely a veneer over the true city. This veil is peeled back as living collages and impossible animals clamber their way through, and the reader is given a glimpse into the blackness beyond. The rich language he uses to describe the impossible and the monstrous makes me appreciate more than ever what little knowledge I can dredge up about the surrealist movement (scraped together from a high school obsession with Max Ernst and a single unit in a third-year art class). The story weaves together a pair of timelines, starting with an impossible state of affairs and showing us how it came to be, the timelines unfolding together with a slow dawning sensation that is eminently satisfying.

But it's apparent throughout that this book is a *novella*: the action, the conflicts, the fights that inevitably will punctuate any narrative of war or hostile

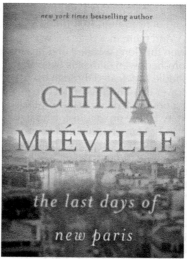

new york times bestselling author

CHINA MIÉVILLE

the last days of new paris

occupation, are given in perfunctory detail and are often anticlimactic. My primary frustration with the story is that it lacks granularity and, therefore, the emotional impact that a good war story should have. There's a contradiction between the action and the indestructibility, as it were, of the main characters, who move from conflict to minor conflict, playing one 'ace card' after another: the book tries to be both a war narrative and a macabre safari and is neither wholly.

The way Miéville disposes of the female character who became my favourite, for example, is downright glib. It's as if he had created an interesting, developed female character by accident, and had now only a limited time left in which to get rid of her. In another example, he builds up a powerful sense of unease around a certain foe, ramping up the action, but we realise that things are not what they seem only a second before the characters themselves do, and so there's none of the tension that makes that kind of revelation so thrilling.

And then, in a page or two, even that long-awaited and heavily foreshadowed climax is over. The baddie is defeated through the power of authorless collective action in a kind of last resort Hail Mary by the protagonist, who until then has largely stumbled from one fight to the next, winning each time through dei ex machina that have more affinity with luck than Thibault's curious affinity for the surreal. This ability of Thibault's to see manifs as they are, and to interact with them, is the most interesting part of his character to my mind and, like Jack Parsons' magical abilities, is not explored in depth.

Which brings me to the problem of the Afterword. All the above were my impressions before reading the afterword, and in light of it my criticisms are arguably unfair. Miéville takes pains to paint himself as a hapless bystander in a story bigger than himself. He's been entrusted with the lost gospel of a forgotten surrealist wartime Paris, and it's his sacred duty to pass it on faithfully.

I want to take the story as it stands, regardless of any context, artificial or otherwise. If the afterword is 'fact', and the meat of *Last Days* – the manifs, the demons, the characters themselves – were given to Miéville by someone else, Miéville himself is absolved from responsibility of any aspect of the story but the cosmetic. My criticism is moot, and we can all go home. If it is all invention, though, then it *is* Miéville's responsibility, and I can't help but see the afterword as a crutch.

It's been suggested to me that I take the afterword as a narrative tool, and appreciate it for its invention, for the way it frames the story. Whether it's true or not is immaterial, though: it still seems like a cop-out, an 'ah-ah, but wait—' before I can make an objection. For want of a better expression, I feel mansplained-to.

Whatever the criticism, *The Last Days of New Paris* is a fascinating piece of writing. Miéville has created a work of remarkable invention in a short space of time. It's the perfect book for someone who already likes Miéville's work, and it's perfect for, say, your former flatmate who did their dissertation on surrealist art. But it's not in-depth enough to really immerse the reader in the way that, say, *Kraken* does and it reads more like a travel journal or a bestiary à la Serafini than a piece of fiction set in wartime Paris.

Raven Stratagem
Yoon Ha Lee
Solaris, 400 pages
Review: Iain Maloney

Criticism is a funny old thing. The critic is late to the party: the book is published, printed, often already in shops and on people's nightstands by the time the review comes out so any criticism offered is at best parenthetical. As a novelist myself I've read critical reviews of my books and thought, 'Okay, so the reviewer thinks W doesn't work, X should've done Y and Z should've been longer. What do they think I can do about it now?' While some writers occasionally get the chance to go back and re-edit older works, the best an author can usually do is to take relevant criticism on board and keep it in mind for the next novel.

This dichotomy was at the front of my mind while reading *Raven Stratagem*, the second part of Yoon Ha Lee's *Machineries of Empire* series, which began with *Ninefox Gambit*. I am a big fan of Lee's writing and thoroughly enjoyed *Ninefox Gambit*, but I never felt quite satisfied. My main beef was the complexity. Lee has created a deeply complex universe, one that in the most fundamental ways is completely alien to us. Not quite parallel, more parabolic. It reminds me, in a good way, of Iain M Banks's Culture in its scope, its pleasing disfunction and the humorous uses Lee makes of the technological and social quirks that rise emergent from the system. But for a lot of *Ninefox Gambit*, it wasn't particularly clear what was going on beyond the immediate action.

Lee, much to his credit, never info-dumps and never engages in a Telladonna (to steal a phrase from the *West Wing Weekly* podcast) by having one character explain everything to another. The book would've been immensely weakened by either of those techniques, and a writer should never give more information than is strictly necessarily, but I couldn't help coming out of *Ninefox Gambit* feeling a little lost. The critic in me wanted Lee to slow down, to let his creation breathe.

Raven Stratagem, in this sense, is a huge leap forward.

In the first book 400-year-old mass murderer Shuos Jedao was grafted onto the mind of Kel Cheris, creating a deadly duo easily

capable of defeating the heretics at the Fortress of Scattered Needles. *Raven Stratagem* picks things up almost immediately. Cheris's mind is dead and Jedao has hijacked her body, using it to take control of a Kel ship in which he goes haring across the galaxy repelling Hafn invaders and antagonising the ruling Hexarchate, all the while clearly up to something. Jedao is a wonderful fictional creation, a total psychotic bastard you can't help but root for. The sense of pleasure Lee clearly takes in writing about Jedao's villainy again puts me in mind of Iain M Banks. If you like your universes with a dark sense of humour and a wonky moral compass, Lee may be the best thing to happen to Space Opera since Banks's untimely passing.

The novel opens the Hexarchate out, following multiple strands that expand and delineate our understanding while complicating the plot and adding levels that will undoubtedly be explored in later volumes. (Lee's website says 'trilogy' - I hope it's a trilogy in the Douglas Adams sense of the word).

Raven Stratagem is that rare thing – a sequel that betters the original – and is also the most frustrating thing for a reviewer: a book with a plot that cannot be discussed without massive spoilers. But like all great novels, it starts at the end of things. The ruling order that has controlled the galaxy for centuries is on its way out, and something is going to replace it. It could be freedom. It could be chaos. It could be a disaster. From Shoreline of Infinity's base in Scotland, we ask what could be more timely?

Rupert Wong and the Ends of the Earth (Gods and Monsters: Rupert Wong Book 2)
Cassandra Khaw
Abaddon Books, 155 Pages
Review: Benjamin Thomas

Rupert Wong and the Ends of the Earth is the second part of the saga of Rupert Wong, our favorite cannibal chef. While Ends of the Earth is technically a novella, it packs more in its pages than most mammoth tomes we find on the shelves. The tremendous difficulty with novellas for writers is the fact that there are a lot more darlings that have to be killed in order to get the desired word count. Khaw's blade, like the one belonging to her protagonist, is sharp and bloodied. There is nothing in this powerful punch of a story that shouldn't be there and, surprisingly, I was not left holding the frayed strings of a dozen loose ends.

Ends of the Earth picks up after the end of the first novella in the series, Rupert Wong Cannibal Chef. If you haven't read the first part, don't worry, Khaw seamlessly weaves in just enough backstory at just the right moments to give an understanding without dragging the story down.

We follow Rupert from a bloody Beat Bobby Flay / Iron Chef competition where the main ingredients are sautéed eyeballs and browned entrails. Upon completing the contest, Rupert finds himself on the run, driven from where he lives to London where, against both his will and better judgement, he is press-ganged into the Greek pantheon. And, while guts and gore may be his specialty when he's serving them, there's a hint of compassion when he realises not all delicacies start as willing sources of food. But this humane revelation doesn't come without a price. Gods are at war and Rupert must quickly find out if he's 100% smart-ass or if he has some

GODS & MONSTERS
RUPERT WONG
AND THE ENDS OF THE EARTH
CASSANDRA KHAW
'She's too good a writer to ignore.' Chuck Wendig

courage buried in his spinal cord.

Khaw hooked me from the beginning with her writing and I feel compelled to inject a paragraph of her descriptive power because it is just that good:

Orpheus is a literal head *on the seat of his wheelchair, the stump of his throat putrid, purple-blotched. A tangle of nerves worm from beneath the flaps of his skin, knotting in the wheels, crawling over the armrests. I suspect that's how he moves around but I'm not going to ask because frankly, I think I've hit my daily foot-in-mouth quota.*

Khaw covers the better side of the Greek Pantheon in her story and expands on a world she introduced in the first Rupert Wong novella. Some of the gods and goddesses I remembered from history class, but not knowing all of them didn't detract from the story at all. The characters are written in such a way that everyone belongs and nothing is out of place or feels forced in order to crowbar in a particular deity's name.

As I said before: there is nothing in this story that shouldn't be here and I strongly recommend picking it up to bring some color to the morning or afternoon commute. Of course, as with all cannibal cook-offs, that color's going to be red.

Ancestral Machines, A Humanity's Fire Novel
Michael Cobley
Orbit, 504 pages
Review: Duncan Lunan

I enjoyed the *Humanity's Fire* trilogy which preceded this novel, but I was concerned that the opening of the Well into vast sub-layers of alternative realities and ancient technologies would submerge the emphasis on human values which had characterised the early parts of the trilogy. When I found that *Ancestral Machines* begins down there, I feared that my misgivings would be justified – intriguing though it was to find events in "a cavernous opening half a million miles wide and about three million long, its floor a vast plain littered with the cracked, smashed and split ruins of entire worlds", like Slartibardfast's workshop in the film version of *Hitchhiker...* if the antigravity failed. I was also put off by starting with a conversation between two artificial intelligences, of which I have been reading rather a lot in recent SF. However, the action moves from there up to our level of reality, the prime continuum, and though the drone which is dispatched to it has a major part to play towards the end, it's out of action for much of the novel.

It's sent to counter the emergence near 'Earthsphere' of a truly nasty construct called the Warcage, which was once an artificial solar system called the Great Harbour of Benevolent Harmony. It has long since been taken over by dissidents with a lust for war and conquest, who pit the inhabitants of its planets against one another, breeding ever more savage warriors, and replacing each world as it becomes ruined with a fresh one stolen from elsewhere. Such planet-collecting has featured in SF before, in the BBC's long-forgotten serial *The Big Pull*, in a story by the late Lesley Hatch called 'Asset-strippers' in the *Daily Record*'s 'Lance McLane

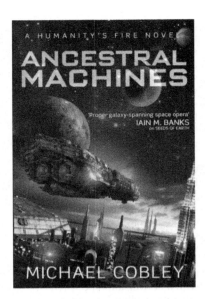

'Proper galaxy-spanning space opera'
IAIN M. BANKS
on SEEDS OF EARTH

strip', and in *Doctor Who*. Until recently the general view in astrodynamics was that such collections of habitable worlds were dynamically impossible, and it's described here as "a massive macro-engineering achievement", although the late Prof. Archie Roy wasn't so sure – simulations at Glasgow University had suggested that up to 60 earthlike worlds could be added to the inner Solar System without drastic effect. The recent discovery of seven earthlike planets tightly clustered around the star TRAPPIST-1 suggests that maybe planetary collection could work without super-technology to hold the system together. In that literal sense, the late Chris Boyce may not have been right when he said, "Interstellar chequers is not a viable mode of existence".

The TV/film comparisons are appropriate because in his Acknowledgements Michael Cobley makes a second dedication, to the writers and actors of *Firefly*. Here the freelance starship captain is called Pyke (try not to think of the *Star Trek* pilot episode or of *Dad's Army*, and when he meets up with a woman officer of Earthspace intelligence called Sam, try not to think of *Stargate*). We meet him when he's just been robbed of a cargo and two of his crew have (apparently) been killed. Setting off in pursuit, he rescues another, stranded crew who take over the ship. To regain it and crew members being held hostage, he must penetrate the Warcage and assassinate a local overlord, to give rebellion against them time to find its feet.

That's only a partial summary and there are numerous complicating elements, particularly a military leader on the other side who's haunted by the personalities of his ancestors – at first an irritation but later to prove crucial. It's all good rollicking stuff, and the few reservations I have concern characterisation and plot. I think Michael relies too much on reader knowledge of *Firefly* to let us link to his characters. The series is not that well known – it was just a word to me until *Serenity* was televised, amd not having the background, it meant little to me then. I wouldn't have seen it now, but that my wife is a fan of Nathan Fillion in *Castle*. And while I can see him as 'Mal' Reynolds haring off after his missing cargo and revenge, for dramatic reasons within an episode, it's at least possible (especially at movie length) that he would cut his losses, bide his time, and position himself for a more satisfying retribution. Like the one in Tom Toner's *The Promise of the Child*, which I reviewed here in Issue No. 2, the whole assassination plot rests on similar shaky assumptions throughout. In particular, I can't see Reynolds letting *Firefly* be taken over by strangers with such laughable ease: all it takes is for the last two crew members aboard Pyke's ship to be given a false message that they're wanted at the base of the ramp.

Starting a story *in medias res* is a powerful device, but it's not always effective. Pyke loses two of his crew at the outset, more are taken hostage as he loses his ship, and on his way into the Warcage still another has to be left behind at a location which proves crucial later. I regret to say that I began to find this funny rather than sharing Pyke's anger and grief, let alone the feelings of the other crew members, and when they're reunited at the end I didn't rejoice as I should, because I'd never seen them working together as a team in the first place. But now they are all back together and have their ship back, no doubt there will be more fun to come.

The List
Patricia Forde
Sourcebooks Jabberwocky, 368 pages
Review: Katie Gray

In the city of Ark, food, water and words are tightly rationed. The world as we know it has ended, the sea levels have risen, and in the last known bastion of civilisation the people must speak the new language, List, or be expelled into the forest. Care of the List, some five hundred words and falling, is in the hands of the city wordsmith, Benjamin, and his apprentice Letta.

One day Benjamin sets out into the wilderness on a routine word-finding expedition – and never returns. Left alone, Letta takes in an injured boy, Marlo, who she soon realises is one of the Desecrators, a mysterious band of terrorists who seek to take down Ark and List. And of course, through Marlo Letta begins the process of unlearning the truths she's been taught her whole life.

Billed as *Fahrenheit 451* meets *The Giver*, *The List* (first published as *The Wordsmith* in 2015) doesn't quite live up to that pedigree, but it's an enjoyable read with a strong, simple message: language is vital, art is vital, and their destruction is the destruction of humanity itself. There's something to be said for this clarity of moral purpose, especially in the current political climate – sadly, *The List*'s central anti-authoritarian, anti-propaganda themes resonate more strongly now that on its initial publication.

The city of Ark and the daily lives of its residents are sketched very well, its infrastructure and logistics, and in particular the work of the wordsmiths. They collect and compile words, recording them in a card catalogue for preservation. Special lists are produced for people in technical professions; 'pumped' is reserved for those who work with water. When a citizen of Ark grows old, they sometimes 'donate' their words to the wordsmith. Speaking non-List words is illegal: fifteen infractions and you'll be exiled.

Unfortunately, the wider world of *The List* is less convincing. There's just enough information given about the history of Ark to make it implausible. A little less, and one could accept this new status quo at face value, but as it is I struggled to believe that anyone would really go along with List. Ark's founder, John Noa, believed that language was the root of humanity's evil. This is, to put it bluntly, patently bonkers. Do the people of Ark really believe him? Are they playing along out of fear? Some combination of the two? It's never properly explained, and Letta's faith in Noa, so central to the novel, isn't fully convincing.

There are also hints throughout the novel of a romance brewing between Letta and Marlo, which I found somewhat unnecessary. They have little in the way of genuine, person-to-person interaction, and I didn't feel much chemistry. If the romance was intended, it isn't convincing, and it feels – as is too often the case – that as male and female leads of *course* they must be paired up. Also, must we really be reminded every time he appears that Marlo smells like sage?

Those issues aside, *The List* is an enjoyable novel with an intriguing premise, a solid moral message, and some great world-building. I don't know if Patricia Forde has plans for a sequel, but I would absolutely read one – it would be great to see this world and its characters developed further.

Stranger of Tempest
Tom Lloyd
Gollancz, 472 pages
Review: Ian Hunter

With ringing endorsements from the likes of Adrian Tchaikovsky, James Barclay and Edward Cox, and a great cover by Jon McCoy, of a lone rifleman (actually our hero armed with a Mage Gun that fires elemental bullets) about to square off to something that looks more than slightly like the Balrog from *Lord of the Rings*, you know you are going to be in safe hands with the first instalment of Lloyd's *The God Fragments* entitled *Stranger of Tempest*.

We are dropped straight into the action as we join Lynx, a mercenary and his merry band who are about to rescue of a damsel in distress. Unfortunately, despite being naked and in some peril, this is no damsel and she's more likely to cause distress to others. This is just the last thing that world-weary Lynx needs, although he could have probably picked less colourful mercenaries to join up with in the first place. This lot are led by Atanin, the Prince of Sun, and resemble a biker gang, some of whom get to wear a jacket depicting a card from a pokerish sort of card game. This results in gang members with names like Prince of Sun, Knight of Blood and Stranger of Tempest. Before we get to the aforementioned rescue

Knights Charnel. The only way they can escape alive will be to travel through some abandoned tunnels – abandoned, for good reason.

Given that Lloyd has written eight previous novels, he is an old hand at world building. His creation is multilayered with its own rules and hierarchy and magical systems. There is the usual smattering of religious and political intrigue and since this is the first in a series we are on a need to know basis with reveals happening throughout the novel. We are given only tantalising mentions of the God Fragments and glimpses of creatures like the Elementals. Like some of the best books of this kind, Lloyd treats us to action, humour and lively banter between the mercenaries. Lynx has a few secrets of his own up his sleeve, or in what is left of his heart.

The God Fragments ends with some promo details about other Lloyd novels and an extract from his e-book only novella called *Honour Under Moonlight!* which takes place just a few weeks after *Stranger of Tempest* finishes and before the next novel *Princess of Blood* appears this summer. While *Stranger of Tempest* could be read as a stand alone novel, I suspect many readers will be dipping into that e-novella and joining that Princess in a few months time. I might too.

of the damsel we helpfully get a table showing the mercenary deck of cards ranging from Sun, Stars, Blood, Snow and Tempest, and the face cards made up of Prince, Knight, Diviner, Stranger, Madman and Jester. In the gang Lynx has joined, some of these positions are empty, and unnamed. Whether or not any of them get filled will depend on how long the group can stay alive. They have rescued a female night mage who was held captive and are on the run from her captors – a bunch of religious fanatics called the

A world of enjoyment in

ORKNEY *International*
SCIENCE FESTIVAL

7 - 13
S E P
2017

more
than 60
events
Sailing by the Sunstone
Peter Higgs In Conversation
The Musical Fireman and the Stars
Dragon in the Darkness
Gravitational Waves and Island Links
Big Bill and the Guns of Alamein
The Sultan and the Stars
The Mystery Lights of Hessdalen
Island Stargazing
The Aurora Man

More Information on
www.oisf.org
www.frontiersmagazine.org

Multiverse

Russell Jones

Praise the merciful overlords; we've been given more space for SF poetry! To celebrate their benevolence, I present the work of (not two, but) three poets. As our tentacled masters demand, here are a few words to guide your ship in to dock…

"Extraterrestrial" by Lauren Harwyn follows a vicious life-form as it eats up star systems, feeding on pain. A relationship gone very sour indeed! Harwyn's "When Bride Came" recounts the life of a traveller, god-like in the eyes of the sick and needy, building a world she doesn't want to abandon.

Louise Peterkin's "Pulses" blends gardening with natal alien growths to produce a verse of half-nightmare, half-serenity. Then, "My Father's Sci-Fi", a prose poem, reminisces about the great and good of SF, which slowly dissolves into something more sinister. Be careful, folks, SF can have harmful side-effects!

"Spring Offensive" by Colin McGuire considers the alienating effects of the changing seasons and years, electrified by airs of violence, rebellion and nihilism. Finally, McGuire's "Juno" follows the NASA spacecraft on its flight to Jupiter, as if attending a wedding. But what does the future hold for a commitment spanning 1.74 billion miles?

Extraterrestrial

I'm too keen for this world.
I devour,
lapping up star systems
like spilled apple pies.
I question your slick grace
with sabre-edged glances—
I know your fantasies,
the way you let them loose
when the moon darkens in January.
I vivisect you, leave you butchered
and clean.
In the long nights, I sing pain,
composing celestial laments
but gravity keeps me.

Lauren Harwyn

When Bride Came

When Bride came, her ship aglow with burning atmosphere,
the crouching, cowering Celts believed she was a god.
When Bride came, an unauthorized traveler,
she placed her protective cloaking device out over the emerald hills.
When Bride came, gold-tongued ambassador of the stars,
poets wove her tripod communicator out of purple reeds.
When Bride came, with her M-class medi-kit,
she had enough vaccines to cure the frail, the sick, the blind.
When Bride came, master engineer, she fixed the broken replicator
and everyone ate cheese.
When Bride came and scanned the geosphere,
her laser drills left deep-cut wells which filled with fresh spring water.
When Bride came, she set a homing beam alight,
so as she wept to leave the earth, she might return again someday.

Lauren Harwyn

Lauren Harwyn is a writing witch and intersectional feminist from California, USA. Harwyn graduated with honors from Mills College, Oakland, CA and attended Scottish Universities' International Summer School for creative writing in Edinburgh, Scotland. She has been published by *Dear Damsels, Zoetic Press, Northern Light*, and elsewhere. Harwyn won Soliloquies Anthology's flash fiction contest and attended the Orchids Without Attached Thighs workshop with Winter Tangerine.

Pulses

We hoped for surfeit, epic globes, a bounty
so ribbed and basketballed,
uprooting it would launch us backwards,
making soil-angels in the rich pudding earth,
clutching the yield to our chests like kids
we had saved from drowning. We trusted
our harvest would be whimsical; carrots
bearded like Border Terriers, veg so fertile
it frowned like a facial composite. To claim
we got the opposite would not be the full story
but we were gloomy then, ambitions of first prize
fete rosettes crumbling as the spade clanged
out another return of dull chaffs
like dried bugs from a family heirloom. For once
we had enjoyed a common goal, a shared hobby.
Had planned, laboured, feeding
our allotted ground with mounds of kelp,
pounded egg shell, dark tea bogged down to molasses.
We stared mournfully at the disturbed plot,
assessing the drab lot at our feet, the conception
that what we had reaped was not what we'd sowed.

That evening we made supper from our gleanings,
joking about sows ears and silk purses,
but were muted as the huge pan bubbled
under the harsh kitchen light.
I held up the crooked husk;
a weird, long, dishwater thing,
knuckled like a finger; new born; senescent. Afterwards
as we lay in bed, I thought of the beans
rolling round our plates, their alien autopsy colour.
It was then I was jolted by an oscillation inside me,
a throb like a smothered orchestra. You stirred
on your side and I placed my splayed palm
across your belly – a middle aged man's paunch,
stretched from years of home brew.
But the swelling felt different:
tighter, somehow significant. And I felt it in you:
that same strange movement, undulation. I timed
our two throbbings till they rhythmed in tandem
then dropped off to a deep sleep, comforted
by our peas-in-a-podness, dreaming of surfeit.

Louise Peterkin

My Father's Sci-Fi

Hard backed, jam-packed in condiment colours: cocktail sauce, Colman's Mustard. A sepia tang rose from inside, pages the colour of old men's fingers. Time travel of deflated prices: 80p for a novel, more in US/Canadian dollars. Kneeling at the shelf behind the sofa I fought the tedium of long afternoons slack as space; the drowsy clock; sear of sad, squandered sun on my back. My father lay dozing. Sometimes, his snoring would stop and I counted the s e c o n d s a sick fear he was dead making my toes tingle. Only his Norse blasts resuming released my own breathing, the task of the antiquarian. Philip K. Dick. Dunes sprawling dynasty. Asimov's mysteries – taut and lovely – a box of gems held up with tweezers in a stark white light, the jeweller a squinting cyclops. I liked Bradbury, collections compiled from 50's magazines. The best story hurled me

like a pod from a spaceship into a vacuum of infinite dark folded onto itself like velvet with absolutely no

stars. A man on a long haul space flight. He was convinced his sole companion, Wilbur, was an android, assigned to save his mind from the crumble of solitary confinement. Wilbur was detached, aloof, impersonal. Our narrator: charismatic, inquisitive, jovial.

Then they switched him off. They. Switched. Him. Off. The narrator was the robot all along.

That was a kick in the guts.

That was when I realised there were stairs in my head and I had to stare straight ahead not to tumble down them, get smashed at the bottom.

The covers were frightening: A prickly jewel stared out from one, a sort of pincushion with eyes hanging in a sea of yellow. The worst was a man with a bald head cracked at the top like a boiled egg, out of which rose a moth. The moth rising out of the man's head had a man's head. And it was bald as an egg, cracked at the top with a moth rising out. The moth had the face of a man's bald egg head, cracked...

Louise Peterkin

Louise Peterkin has had poems featured in various publications including *The Dark Horse, New Writing Scotland* and *The North*. In 2016 she won a New Writers Award for poetry from the Scottish Book Trust.
She lives and works in Edinburgh.

Spring offensive

Spring is here all blasé and the sun storms
the city with its solar weaponry
armed with melanoma in broad daylight.

Are our laptops the gravesites
of long lost flower beds
we could be attending to?

Flowers are pustules, infectious and leaking.
The colours are so violent.
Why do all the beautiful things have cancer?

We tend plastic morning glories,
eat sweeteners and bathe under UV light.
The horizon is the colour of a lit fuse.

We purchase an AI robot as a nanny.
On a busy day, she sighs,
threatens to destroy all of humanity.

Children buy gas masks to see
who can hold their breath longest
before having to strap theirs back on.

We repeat the word equinox
over and over again
until it means nothing.

Colin McGuire

Colin McGuire is a poet and performer from Glasgow, who lives in Edinburgh.
He has written and performed relentlessly over the last fifteen years, and is the
author of three collections, the most recent being his first full collection, As I sit
quietly, I begin to smell burning, (Red Squirrel Press, 2014).
He has also been an ESOL teacher for the last seven years, teaching English to
young learners and adults from across the world.

Juno

Juno is a NASA spacecraft on a mission to the planet Jupiter

A five-year galavant 1.74 billion miles out;
an all-inclusive holiday. Nothing but a speck
on the lens of a microscope.

On your dashboard a plaque bares a dispatch
from Galileo: 'I was the first to see
your four moons, Jove, way back when...'

Three Lego figurines, lucky talismans:
Galileo himself; Jupiter, god of the sky,
and wife Juno, the goddess of marriage.

Good karma tied to the rearview mirror,
Earth, a furry dice, swinging
pendulously in the interior.

Juno, the dune buggy,
off on a road trip to meet
your mysterious other half.

Jupiter is all gas anyway,
but you want to know
what lies behind that giant veil,

if there is any substance beneath that reputation.
You will go as close as you can, park up,
spread your three solar arms wide;

a temporary star,
recording exactly what
we don't know.

You orbit round Jupiter like the first dance
between bride and groom;
and it will all be over, Juno, all too soon.

Colin McGuire

Support

Shoreline of Infinity

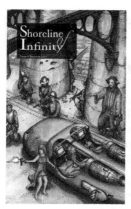

Thank you for buying this issue of Shoreline of Infinity: your purchase goes towards the fees we pay our writers and artists, and towards the costs of running the magazine.

Thank you too for reading this issue of Shoreline of Infinity: by so doing the writers, artists and the editorial team—and we hope you do too—receive a warm fuzzy feeling inside.

As you sit with us around the fire of driftwood, sparks floating to mingle with the stars in the sky, can we ask you do one more small thing? Can we ask you to sponsor Shoreline of Infinity SF magazine?

Here are some of the ways you can do that, and the benefits for you:

Esteemed Reader $1 per month	Hallowed Holder of the Book $5 per month	Potent Protector of the Printed Word $10 per month	Mighty Mentor of the Masterpiece $40 per month
Digital subscription to Shoreline of Infinity quarterly	Print edition subscription to Shoreline of Infinity quarterly	Sponsorship of one story in Shoreline per year	Sponsorship of one Shoreline cover picture per year
Get your copy of Shoreline before the general public sees it	Free postage and packing	The Patron's name published with the story	The Patron's name appears prominently on the back cover
Access to patron-only updates from the Shoreline team	Plus all previous rewards	A certificate identifying the Patron as the sponsor of the story, naming the story and the writer	A high quality print of the cover image suitable for framing
Exclusive access to the Shoreline private forum		Plus all the benefits of an Esteemed Reader	Plus all the benefits of an Esteemed Reader
Your name in our hall of heroes on the Shoreline website		Plus all the benefits of a Hallowed Holder of the Book	Plus all the benefits of a Hallowed Holder of the Book

And there's more. Visit our Patreon page:

www.patreon.com/shorelineofinfinity

And find out how you can help.

Shoreline of Infinity founders
Noel Chidwick, Editor
Mark Toner, Art Director
Edinburgh, Scotland

Flash Fiction Competition for Shoreline of Infinity Readers

Visible from the Shoreline of Infinity Beach Hut HQ are these landscapes illustrated by Becca McCall (below) and Siobhan McDonald. Let these illustrations – singly or together – inspire you to create a story. We're looking for flash fiction, which we're defining as a maximum of 1,000 words.

Just remember, *Shoreline of Infinity* is a science fiction(ish) magazine, and your story must be science-fictional.

Prizes: £40 for the winning story plus 1 year digital subscription to *Shoreline of Infinity*. Two runners-up will receive 1 year digital subscription to *Shoreline of Infinity*.

The top three stories will be published in *Shoreline of Infinity* –

All three finalists will receive a print copy of this edition.

Also

The best stories submitted (up to a maximum of 20,000 words in total) will be published in 2018 in an anthology, and each contributor will receive a digital copy and a pro-rata share of the royalties.

The Detail

Maximum 1,000 words.

Maximum 2 stories per submitter.

Deadline for entries: midnight (UK time) 30th September 2017.

To enter, visit the website at:

www.shorelineofinfinity.com/2017ffc

There's no entry fee but you will be asked for a secret code word only obtainable from reading issue 8 of Shoreline of Infinity.

Lightning Source UK Ltd.
Milton Keynes UK
UKOW05f0058310517

302355UK00002B/111/P